HOT JOCKS 3

TRYING TO SCORE

New York Times & *USA Today* Bestselling Author

KENDALL RYAN

Trying to Score

Developmental Editing

Rachel Brookes

Copy Editing by

Pam Berehulke

Cover Design and Formatting by

Uplifting Author Services

ABOUT THE BOOK

Teddy King excels at many things. Playing hockey. *Check.* Scoring on and off the ice. *Check.* Being stupidly attractive ... *Double check.*

Despite his demanding schedule, he still finds time to annoy me. I knew him way back when. Before he was the guy everyone wanted a piece of, he was just a rebellious college co-ed and one of my more *energetic* study partners.

But secrets have a way of getting out, and a steamy encounter from our college days (that we probably shouldn't have filmed) is about to cause a major scandal. Unless we can work together to stop it.

Teddy's no stranger to hard work … but the thing he wants most?

Is me.

PLAYLIST

"Trouble" by Cage the Elephant

"It's Been Awhile" by Staind

"Leila" by Miami Horror

"You're Somebody Else" by Flora Cash

"Human" by Rag'n'Bone Man

"Love Syndrome" by Enamour

"Him and I" by G-Eazy and Halsey

CHAPTER ONE

Going Once, Going Twice, Sold

Sara

There's a lot a girl could do with five-hundred dollars.

I could easily blow that money splurging on the camel-colored suede boots I've been ogling for the past month but can't justify buying. Or I could book a round-trip flight somewhere warm and take the vacation I desperately need from my ninety-hour workweeks at the law firm. If I wanted to be practical, I could set that money aside in a bank account and watch it earn interest.

But tonight, I gave myself a limit of five-hundred big ones to spend on landing myself an evening with one of the hottest men Seattle has to offer.

Before you go thinking dirty thoughts, no, I

don't mean like *that.*

Every year, a group of us buys a table for the charity date auction put on by the nonprofit my friend Aubree works for. The girls love the excuse to wear fancy dresses, and the guys like that they can drink beer under the guise of doing it "for a cause."

Tonight is our third consecutive year attending, but it's the first year that some of the Ice Hawks players have volunteered to auction themselves off. Teddy, Owen, and a few of the players from the second and third lines I hardly recognize outside the hockey arena are all dressed especially dapper this evening, each one with a YOUR FUTURE DANCE PARTNER button pinned to his lapel to indicate that he's up for auction tonight.

And there's another first this year. It's the first time that I've allowed myself to bid. Work has been beyond stressful since I've started to be considered as a contender for partner at the law firm I've worked for since college. Of course, more responsibility has meant I've been working more hours, so my social life has become practically nonexistent.

Why not spend some of my hard-earned cash on someone tall, dark, and temporary to relieve some of that anxiety? It's for charity, after all. And if a few shared cocktails and slow dances lead to something more? Let's just say, I am here for it. It's been way too long since I've enjoyed a man's company.

"Hey, Becca, do you think I stand a chance of snagging a date with Owen tonight?" Justin asks, raising his brows across the table at Becca, who rolls her eyes in response.

"Better you than one of these superfans." She half scoffs, half giggles. "I'm worried I'm going to have to pull some middle-aged woman's hands off my boyfriend's butt in the middle of a slow dance."

Owen squeezes Becca's hand in reassurance. "Don't worry, babe. You get to keep dating me for free tomorrow."

That idiotic comment only earns him a sappy smile from Becca, and I sigh in exasperation.

Love makes you weird.

Justin takes a swig of beer and directs his attention to Teddy, who's typing furiously on his phone. "What about you, TK? You're up for grabs. Think I can nab you for the evening?"

Teddy King, a six-foot-three-inch wall of muscle with dark wavy hair and captivating green eyes, barely looks up from his phone. He's been on it all night, and to be honest, it's kind of annoying. Tonight is supposed to be a fun night with friends, not an opportunity for him to scroll through social media.

"Is your Instagram feed really that interesting, Teddy?" I say sassily, then sip my vodka soda.

I'm not one to pass up an opportunity to give him grief. We're friends, no question, but he and I also have a bit of a history, which I choose to suppress by directing as many snarky comments his way as possible. His fingers tap angrily at his phone screen. I know from experience the way those thick fingers feel … the way his touch buzzes through my body, but tonight those strong hands won't come anywhere near my bare skin.

"I'm dealing with something, okay?" His grips tightens around the phone and he lowers it, pocketing it beneath the table, as if to shield it from view. Usually, he'll give me shit right back, but tonight, he looks up at me with a blend of alarm and frustration in his eyes.

I tense and lean back, giving him space. I can't ignore the shot of panic that bolts down my spine, though.

It's not like Teddy to be so closed off, especially at an event like this. Normally he's so fun loving, constantly cracking jokes with his teammates, telling funny stories and laughing. Whatever is going on must be serious.

Part of me wants to ask him what's wrong, but his eyes are already locked on his screen again, so I turn my attention back to the stage. Someone has just secured an evening with the quarterback of the Seattle Sirens, and I can't help but feel the slightest pang of jealousy that I didn't bid on that hunky piece of man meat. His broad shoulders look absolutely scrumptious in his fitted charcoal-gray tux. I can't say I would mind clutching those while riding him all night long.

What can I say? I'm a sucker for athletes. In law school, I used to spend all my time studying in the library that overlooked the football field, and ever since, I've had a taste for men who know when to play by the rules and when to break them. The muscles, of course, are also a major selling point. As is their stamina. But it's something about that gleam in their eyes, that competitive spirit that never quite leaves their system. It's such a turn-on in the bedroom.

And that's where I have to keep my affinity for

athletes: in the bedroom, and not a step beyond.

Do you know what happens when you try to mix a lawyer's ninety-hour workweek with an athlete's insane practice schedule and constant travel? Me neither. But I know it can't be good. Which is why I've kept my romantic life strictly between the sheets for the past year or so. Maybe it will be a different story when I become the first female partner at my law firm, but as long as I have something to prove in the office, the only serious relationship I'm allowing myself is with my work email in-box. I'm committed, what can I say?

Next up onstage is an Ice Hawks defenseman the team picked up this year. I can't say I've spoken more than a half dozen words to the guy, but he fills out his suit in all the right ways, and for a moment, I consider putting in a bid. I've got the money to spend, and it's really for two excellent causes: ending childhood hunger, and potentially setting myself up to receive a much-needed orgasm or two tonight from someone other than my vibrator.

Nope, nope, and nope. Check yourself before you wreck yourself, Sara.

I can only imagine the kind of conversations that go down in the Ice Hawks' locker room, and

I'd like to keep the details of my sex life as far away from the guys as possible. As it is, there's already one player who knows a little too much about my likes and dislikes in the bedroom.

The crowd politely claps as the defenseman is auctioned off to a little boy and his mom, who look eager to get an autograph. Totally aw-worthy.

Aubree, who is slaying the role of tonight's em-cee, flips her notes to the next card. "Up next," she says, "is Owen Parrish, the goalie of our very own Seattle Ice Hawks."

The crowd cheers loudly, hooting and hollering for the much-loved star goalie.

As Owen stands to take the stage, Becca jolts up in her seat, throwing a hand in the air and yelling out her $100 bid. Someone immediately out-bids her, and it doesn't take long for Owen's price to climb well over $400. At that point, Becca folds and takes her seat, grumbling and crossing her arms over her chest as Owen finally sells for nearly a grand.

"All that money to dance with Owen for a night?" Elise laughs. "I should show those wom-en the video of him as a sheep in our elementary school Christmas pageant. The way he head-butted the angels during the big dance number would have them retracting their bids."

"Sounds baaaaaaaaa-d." Justin bleats, sending the whole table into giggles, Becca included.

"Speaking of bad," Teddy whispers soft enough that only I can hear him. "Can we talk? We have a little bit of a situation on our hands."

My brow creases as I appraise him. *We? Our?*

Teddy and I haven't been a "we" since back in college. And even then, barely. We traded study notes and orgasms one semester before deciding we were better off as friends. It wasn't even a big enough deal for us to tell our friend group about. What could possibly have him referring to us as a singular unit again?

"Now?" I whisper back, my eyes widening slightly. "Is it urgent?"

He gives me a firm nod. "I'd say it's mega urgent."

I glance around the hotel ballroom we're in, looking for somewhere he and I can have a private conversation. We don't have a ton of options without leaving the room altogether. Looks like I'm going to have to improvise.

"Bar. Now," I whisper.

I make an excuse to the table about my vodka soda being too watered down and head for the bar. A few seconds later, Teddy stands up to join me.

As he walks my way, I can't resist doing a once-over of his sculpted frame. I won't lie, he's hotter than sin, all of his muscles fully on display in that well-fitted tux. I mentally high-five College Sara for her good taste in sex partners.

"What's going on?" I ask when he sidles up beside me, a frown etched across his full mouth.

"I just received a really threatening email." Teddy's green eyes cloud over with worry. "I think someone is trying to blackmail me. Which means I'm probably going to need a damn good lawyer, right?"

"Not probably. Definitely. I think I might know a good lawyer," I tease, gesturing to myself. It was an attempt to lighten the mood, but the worry in Teddy's eyes doesn't let up, so I return to the issue at hand. "What kind of blackmail are they implying?"

He doesn't have time to give me an answer before we're interrupted by Aubree, continuing her emcee duties.

"We have one more date up for auction tonight. Our last hockey hottie of the evening, Teddy King."

Teddy sighs. "I guess that's my cue." He forces a lighthearted smile as he smooths his dark hair with one hand and turns toward the stage.

Hopefully the rest of the guests can't see through his strained smile the way I can. Whatever this email is about, it's affecting him in a major way.

As I watch him onstage, I mentally catalog his attributes. He has the body of an athlete, that's for sure. Tall. Broad shoulders. Trim waist. His hair is slightly disheveled from his roaming fingers, but it's oddly endearing. There's normally a playful look in his eyes, a smile that signals he's ready for trouble, but tonight his look is somber, and I'm not sure what to make of that.

"Shall we start the bidding at two hundred?"

A bidder jumps in right away, then another and another until his going price is up to $500, the max budget I set for myself tonight. But I missed my opportunity to bid on the quarterback while being distracted with Teddy at the table, so I might as well save him from his own fake smile.

"One thousand dollars." I raise my hand in the

air, almost not recognizing my own voice when I bid.

Did I really just freaking do that?

Everyone at my table turns and gives me a dumbfounded look, and I can hardly keep my poker face in place.

Why the hell did I bid a grand to have a conversation with Teddy that we're obviously going to have either way? Maybe because he said it was mega urgent? Maybe it was the worry in his voice? With the bid I just placed, I guess I'm hoping he wasn't exaggerating.

"Going once? Going twice?" Aubree sweeps her glance over the room. "Sold, for a thousand dollars to my friend Sara Dawson." She grins at me from the stage.

One thousand dollars. Twice my budget for the precise opposite of the date I was looking to snag tonight. This man owes me big-time, literally a grand's worth.

I lift the hem of my red satin dress so I don't trip in my heels on the walk up to the stage to claim my prize. Teddy King, a.k.a. TK, a.k.a. my college fling who I just dropped a grand on for what better be a damn good reason.

As the other winning couples filter out onto the dance floor, I spot Owen with his flirty forty-something date, with Becca watching like a hawk from a few feet away. A few of the other guys are signing autographs for some kids, and Elise is congratulating Aubree on her awesome job emceeing. Everyone is distracted, giving Teddy and me the perfect opportunity to slip away and hash out this blackmail situation.

"Thanks for bidding on me," Teddy says, scrubbing his fingers through his hair as we duck out of the ballroom and into an adjacent conference room. It's empty, of course, just a large conference table and a half dozen rolling chairs. "I was worried I was going to look like a second stringer if Owen sold for more than I did."

"Your ego wasn't my concern," I say, clicking the door shut behind us. "I'm a bit more worried about this email situation."

The smile on Teddy's lips falls away. "Yeah, about that. The sender of the email is saying they've hacked into my cloud. And they've gotten their hands on a certain video and are threatening to release it."

My eyebrows scrunch together. "What video?"

There's a moment of silence as Teddy swallows, his eyes narrowing into a meaningful stare. "*The* video."

Two words. That's all it takes to drain all the blood from my face.

I steady myself, bracing one hand on the conference table until I can lower myself into a seat. *The* video? That can't be possible. This has to be some kind of sick joke. The vodka soda in my stomach sours.

"I don't understand. We deleted every single copy of that video back in college."

Teddy hangs his head, fisting his hands into his pockets. "Yeah, I know I said that. But I may have, you know, held on to one personal copy—for sentimental reasons."

My chest tightens as all the air in my lungs disappears. "Why the hell would you do that?"

"I know, I'm sorry. It's my bad." He sounds sincere, but when he finally looks up at me, there's a hint of uncertainty on his face. "It's just . . . that shit was hot, you know? That was my first and only sex tape, Sara. I couldn't just delete it."

What the actual hell?

If I didn't have such good self-control, I would be strangling him with the strap of my purse right now. Teddy promised me years ago that every trace of that video had been wiped out, deleted, never to be seen again. And now some creepy hacker dude has his grubby hands on it and is threatening to release it? How long until it's plastered onto websites around the globe? We'll both be completely ruined.

My heart hammers against my ribs, and I feel like punching something.

There must be steam coming out of my ears, because Teddy starts laying the apologies on thick. "Listen, Sara. I'm sorry. *So* fucking sorry. I didn't mean to betray your trust like that. It's just I never thought it would get out."

I swear I can hear my pulse rioting in my veins, but as it gets progressively louder, I realize it's someone knocking at the door.

"Hey, lovebirds," a familiar voice calls. *Owen.* "I've got something for you." He slips something small and silver beneath the door. A condom.

Freaking great. Now our friends think we're hooking up.

And unless we can stop this creepy computer genius snooping through Teddy's in-box, they're going to have video evidence soon.

CHAPTER TWO

Is It Hot in Here?

Teddy

Undercurrents of tension filled with raw sexuality snap between us. My gaze meets Sara's, and six thousand different emotions slam through me all at once.

I feel like the world's biggest asshole. No, I *am* the world's biggest asshole.

Not only did my messed-up decision to keep a copy of that hot-as-fuck sex tape put Sara's entire future in jeopardy, but I've basically just admitted to the fact that she's been in regular rotation in my spank bank for years. And considering we've kept things strictly platonic for the past seven years now, I know I've caught her totally off guard.

Am I proud of the fact that I regularly jack off

to memories of our hookup? *No*. Has that even once stopped me? *Nope.*

Fuck, I'm the actual worst.

There are many things I know about the woman standing in front of me. She's funny. Smart. Articulate. A kick-ass attorney. But there are other things too… And unfortunately, the thing that lodges in my brain is the *least* helpful right now. Back in college, she majored in Poli Sci and minored in riding my dick. At least junior year. After that, we successfully swerved into the friend zone—which seems like a small miracle given the amount of chemistry zapping between us. It would also help immensely if I didn't still have vivid mental images of plowing into her from behind.

Her lush pink mouth falls open and she makes a breathless sound. It takes me right back to the night everything changed.

We'd been hanging out for a couple of months by then after meeting in a business management lecture at our university. I'd been attracted to her from day one, but since a full course load and playing college hockey kept me busy, and because she'd let it slip that the only committed relationship she was looking for was one with her vibrator and her classes, I'd let it drop. She was smart, pretty, and funny—but I had no time for a girlfriend, and so into the friend zone we ventured. But then one night, things shifted.

It was late. Dark outside. We were wrestling for the remote control on my dorm-room bed after finishing a study session. She ended up in my lap, her hips bumping mine, and then it was game over for my libido. And there was no hiding it. I knew the second she felt my body's physical reaction to hers, because she halted stiffly in my arms, her lips parting in surprise.

"Sorry." I apologized hoarsely, reaching down to adjust the obvious erection bulging in the front of my athletic shorts.

Sara's eyes met mine, then ventured briefly down to my mouth. She didn't climb from my lap or push away from me like I was expecting. Instead, she bit down on her lip, those perfectly straight white teeth chewing on her plump lower lip while she gazed at me.

"Sorry for what?" Her voice had a playful lilt to it.

She had to know, right?

I cleared my throat, willing my erection to fade. "For getting excited. There's a hot chick in my lap, in case you didn't notice," I said, trying to lighten the mood with a smirk.

"Yeah?" she said coyly, still watching me like I was the most fascinating creature in the world. "Do I get you excited, TK?" Her lips twitched with a smile while she waited for my answer.

I was completely out of my element. Her brazen confidence, her directness—it was a lot for twenty-one-year-old me to handle. I was used to shy fumbling in the dark, stolen kisses, and quick hookups that were over almost before they started. This entire conversation felt like foreplay, and I was more turned on than I'd ever been. And she hadn't even laid a single finger on me.

Her challenging stare made me bold, and so I rocked my hips—just once—letting her feel my full arousal and the answer to that question.

"I think that's a big fucking *yes*, don't you?" When her mouth opened again, I was afraid I'd gone too far, and so I mumbled, "But we're friends. So, like I said, I'm sorry."

She cocked her head. "We are friends, but . . . I like sex. You like sex. It's an excellent form of aerobic activity. Not to mention stress relief."

I swallowed the giant lump in my throat. Was

she suggesting what I thought she was suggesting?

There was no way I was that lucky.

"Why don't we just fuck and get it out of the way?" she said in a challenging tone, her sultry blue eyes dancing mischievously at me.

I was sure she was kidding. Fucking with me. She had to be.

Except . . . she wasn't.

That was how we ended up naked in my bed for the first time.

Sara was so spontaneous, so fun, and she loved sex as much as I did. After that first time, it became a regular thing. We were kind of insatiable for each other, hooking up whenever we had free time—after class, late at night, once in the back of the library.

One night I suggested on a whim that we film it, and then waited for her to shoot down the idea. Only she didn't. When she got a flirty gleam in her eye, I started begging, and she laughed at me.

"Please. No one will see it but us," I promised, pinning her down on the bed with my body on top of hers.

She was still smiling when I told her it would get me through the summer and give me something to remember her by. She was leaving in a few days to go back home, a few hours away, where she had an internship lined up at a law office for the summer.

"You won't show any of your teammates?" she asked, searching my eyes.

"God, no," I assured her. "It'll be for our eyes only. I promise."

It wasn't serious between us, but it was monogamous, and I would never share something so private with anyone—let alone my loudmouthed teammates.

It was all the reassurance she needed, because then she helped me set up the camera phone to capture our best (and dirtiest) angles.

The video was scorching hot, and I took great care to save it somewhere no one would ever stumble across it.

But then she called in a panic a few days later, asking me to delete all traces of the video. I calmed her down, promising that I would. And I really intended to. I should have, obviously.

But I couldn't quite bring myself to do it, and so I ended up saving a copy on my personal cloud.

Sara came back to campus the next fall with a new boyfriend she'd met at the law firm, another intern, and that was the end of our physical relationship. We've remained friends, but I never forgot about our hot campus history, or the chemistry that still crackles between us whenever she's near, even all these years later.

And looking at her now, at all those curves draped in red silk, how can I ever forget what we shared? She's a smart, fierce, driven lawyer and, honestly, quite a fucking catch.

But with her demanding career and my pro hockey schedule, it just wasn't meant to be. We both work too much, and plus I'm pretty sure she still sees me as an immature coed jock—the one who suggested sex tapes and library romps and played too many video games—even if I have changed. At least a little.

Sara makes a low noise of disapproval and pulls open the door to the conference room to face our unwelcome intruder.

Owen stands in the hall, his grin fading as he takes in our tense expressions.

"Thought you sneaked away for some fun with your date," he says, meeting Sara's eyes.

"Not hardly." She takes a step forward, obviously ready to set him straight, but my hand on her lower back stops her. She takes a deep breath, composing herself, while I usher Owen into the hallway.

We've never told our friends about our brief history, and honestly, why would we? It's no one's business but our own, and besides, it's ancient history at this point anyway, not exactly breaking news. Unless this fuckface who is threatening to release the video actually does, then it'll be on every news outlet from here to China.

Fuck.

"I need to talk with Sara. In private," I say sternly.

Owen holds up both hands. "It's cool. I was just messing with you."

I nod. "I know. But now's not a good time."

Owen's normally playful expression falls. "Is everything okay?"

"Yeah. All good," I lie. "Just something Sara and I need to work out."

"Cool. Well, if you need me, I'll be eating about six thousand of those crab-puff things. Have you had one? They're amazing." Owen bumps his fist against mine, and then I watch him walk away toward the ballroom before I reenter the conference room and close the door again.

Sara's seated in one of the chairs, looking like she's ready for corporate battle. A worried crease has formed between her brows, the only indication of stress in her otherwise confident demeanor. Another pang of regret that I've put her in this situation jolts through me.

I take the seat across from her and meet her steely blue gaze. "So, will you be my lawyer or not?"

Her features relax, and she lifts her chin. "Doesn't sound like I have a choice."

Releasing a long sigh, I push both hands into my hair. "I'm so fucking sorry about all of this, Sara."

"You apologized already. Twice," she points out.

"That doesn't make it any better." And it certainly doesn't erase the gnawing guilt eating a hole inside my chest.

She frowns. "No, it doesn't. But what's done is done. I guess now we have to face the consequences."

I swallow a lump in my throat. "I never thought that video would get out."

"That makes two of us." Rising to her feet, she steadies herself with one hand on the table. "I don't really feel up to celebrating tonight. I think I'm actually going to head out. We can talk about this tomorrow."

I rise to my feet along with her. "How did you get here?"

"An Uber," she says.

"Then let me drive you home. It's the least I can do."

She doesn't put up a fight, and together we say good-bye to everyone still left at the table. Becca pries away a plate of crab puffs from Owen, telling him he's going to have a stomachache later if he doesn't stop. Normally, this would be comical to watch, but my tense nerves won't let me enjoy their playful squabble.

The car ride is a silent one, and when Sara and I reach her place, I get out and walk her to the front door. We pause together, Sara's eyes on mine, but her expression is impossible to read. I'm afraid I've fucked up beyond repair. And even if we're not romantically involved, I value our friendship above everything else.

"We'll figure this out, okay? Please don't hate me," I say, attempting a smile, but it feels strange, almost like I've forgotten how in the stress of the past few hours.

She shakes her head slightly. "I don't hate you. I knew what I was doing when I said yes to filming us. This just sucks."

"That it does." I rub one hand over the back of my neck. "But I should have deleted the video like you asked." *Understatement of the century.*

She meets my eyes, weighing my words. "Obviously."

"I never showed it to a soul, I promise you. It was just for me. My eyes only." My admission comes out soft and sorrowful, and she has every right to knee me in the nuts right now, but thankfully, for the boys' sake, she doesn't.

Adjusting the strap of her purse on her shoulder, she nods in agreement. "I believe you. And I'm going to work hard to make this thing disappear.

Our first step will be to send a cease-and-desist order."

My relief is immediate and I give a tight nod. "Sounds like a plan. And thanks again."

I pull her into my arms for a hug. Her forgiving reaction and willingness to help makes me feel even worse. She really is an amazing girl, and I hate that I've put her in a bad situation. The hug only lasts for a few seconds, but the simmering attraction I normally keep on lockdown lingers long after I release her.

As I watch her walk inside, I fight to ignore the accompanying twitch in my pants. That's what got us into trouble in the first place, and the last thing I need to do is make everything ten times worse by fondling my attorney.

No matter how badly I might want to.

CHAPTER THREE

Skin in the Game

Sara

After the craziness of law school and an even crazier career as an attorney, I consider myself somewhat of an expert on balancing a packed schedule. My number one tip? Find a friend who is just as busy as you are. Someone who understands that, while you may not get to hang out all the time, your time together is sacred and special. For me, that someone is Bailey. She's literally the best human.

This morning, while most of the girls here at our favorite brunch spot are ordering bottomless mimosas, we're clinking together our coffee mugs and commiserating over the fact that weekends don't really mean downtime for us. With her med school midterms approaching, Bailey is spending this rare time not studying by talking about, well, studying.

How this girl balances med school, work, and any semblance of a social life is beyond me. I barely had enough time to grocery shop back when I was in law school. Actually, scratch that. I barely have enough time to grocery shop now either. Thank God for the new grocery-delivery service I discovered.

"So," Bailey exhales, having shared her entire study schedule with me in an hour-by-hour breakdown, "that's what the next week of my life is going to look like. Do you think I can survive?"

I spread a thin layer of grape jelly onto my toast, thankful for her friendship and the fact that she's doing a pretty decent job of distracting me from this crazy sex-tape drama. "If anyone can survive this, it's you." I meet her eyes with a quick smile. "And hey, at least the auction event is over. That's one less thing on your schedule."

Bailey sighs as she tears open a packet of sweetener and empties it into her mug. "It was a fun event, and I'm glad I got to go. But, honestly, the date auction just reminded me of how long it's been since I've gone on one."

I can totally relate to that. It's been months since I've been out on a proper date. Unless you count winning Teddy at the auction. But I don't think it counts as a date if the main topic of discussion is legal action. In fact, I think that was the first client meeting I've ever *paid for* instead of *being paid.*

"I'm with you on the dating front," I say, dabbing the crumbs off of my lip gloss with a napkin. "Until I make partner, I'm not even thinking about anything that's more than purely physical."

Bailey groans. "I don't even know that I have time for that, though. Finding someone to have sex with means hours of weeding through weirdos on dating apps just to find someone halfway decent. It's practically another homework assignment."

I chuckle into my coffee mug. She's right.

"You could always meet someone in one of your classes," I remind her.

My memory flashes back to that lecture hall back in college, the one where my business management class met. When Teddy sat next to me on the first day, his broad shoulders draped in his hockey jersey and his dark hair still wet from showering after practice, I knew right away that I had found both my study buddy and my fuck buddy for the semester. The sex was adventurous and seriously hot, and I've been chasing athletes ever since, desperately looking for the same rush TK gave me every time he took me to bed.

"Do you think that's smart?" Bailey asks.

I tilt my head, racking my brain for what our topic of conversation was. Med school? Midterms? Whatever it was, my Teddy-inspired daydream threw me off my train of thought.

"Mixing sex and med school," Bailey says. "If I sleep with a guy in my program, I'm worried it could be a distraction."

I stifle my grin with another bite of toast, thinking about how little studying TK and I got done that semester. It's a wonder either of us passed that class. "Great point. Nothing good ever comes out of mixing work and play."

Bailey lifts an eyebrow in my direction. "Why does it sound like you're speaking from experience?"

"I've just heard stories from people I went to law school with," I lie, doing my best to avoid making direct eye contact.

I desperately wish I could tell her every detail about Teddy, the sex tape, the hacker, the whole disaster unfolding before me. But what good is that going to do? Bailey doesn't need any additional worries or anxiety on her shoulders, especially with her exams approaching. And he and I certainly don't need to get more people involved in this mess. What I need to do is talk to Teddy, agree to take his case, and get to work making sure this sex tape is deleted once and for all.

As we wrap up brunch and take care of the check, Bailey suggests continuing our girls' day with pedicures. As good as a nice soak and scrub would be for my mental health, I know I can't put off talking to Teddy any longer.

"I have a really big client meeting," I explain. It's not a complete lie. I'm just leaving out the part where I made a sex tape with said client. And the part where I'm trying to keep that sex tape off of every tabloid website in the world. No pressure.

"No worries. I should be studying anyway." Bailey sighs, her eyes clouding over as she returns to med-school mode. "I wish I could just fast forward to my clinicals already. Or better yet, to the part where I'm an actual doctor."

"The hard work is going to pay off," I assure

her.

It's a good reminder for both of us. Sometimes, it feels like the hours I've been putting in at the firm lately are stripping me of my sanity. Throw in this sex-tape snafu, and I'm a perfect candidate for a complete and total mental breakdown. But if I can keep my nose to the grindstone, I know it will all pay off. I'll earn that corner office, no matter how much sleep I lose or tears I shed along the way.

Once Bailey and I have said our good-byes and I'm in the privacy of my own car, I pull my phone from my purse and press the call button next to Teddy's name. He picks it up right before the call goes to voice mail.

"What's up, Sara?" His voice still has that same nervous tinge from the night of the auction, but now it's paired with a hint of sleepiness that I find strangely appealing.

"Did I wake you up?" I ask, eyeing the time on my car stereo. It's almost eleven a.m.

"It's my morning off," he says. "But no worries. I was going to get up soon anyway."

I roll my eyes, biting my tongue before I can tease him about sleeping so late. If it were any other day, I would show no mercy in ragging on him for his laziness, but there's no time for that right now. We need to cut to the chase and get to work.

"Get a pot of coffee going, would you? I'm coming over, and I have a feeling that neither of us are going to be getting much sleep the next few nights."

Teddy's chuckle is soft and suggestive. "Is that so, baby?" His voice is dripping with sexual undertones.

Seriously? He's going to be flirty with me at a time like this? I scoff, ready to hang up on him, but then he backtracks.

"Wait, I'm sorry. Habit. I'll knock it off. Promise."

"That's more like it," I snap.

This isn't going to work unless he treats this as a professional relationship between lawyer and client. Especially because hearing his raspy voice call me *baby* stirred up something between my legs that I'll never admit to. And that's a road we can't afford to go down because it's what got us into this trouble in the first place.

Just like I told Bailey, nothing good ever comes from mixing work and play.

It's a short drive downtown to Teddy's place, but it always takes a while to find parking. It's probably the only downside of his apartment. In the heart of the city, between all the best clubs and restaurants, stands the glass-and-steel skyscraper he calls home. Thirty floors of Seattle's wealthiest, with Teddy's place at the very top.

I've been here plenty of times before for poker nights, but my jaw still drops a little every time I step into the sleek, all-white lobby. The white marble floors sparkle beneath my tan espadrilles as I walk up to the counter and slip security my driver's license, letting them know who I'm here to see. They check my credentials and buzz up to confirm with Teddy that he's expecting company before handing back my identification and ushering me toward the private elevator that leads to the penthouse.

That's right. Penthouse. With a salary well over six million a year, Teddy King cuts no corners when it comes to his luxury lifestyle.

As the elevator surges upward, the details of this hacker problem start to come together in my head. Of course. I'll bet whoever is torturing him via email thinks that Teddy will drain his bank accounts to make this little problem go away. Which he could do. Not that it would stop this creep from leaking the video regardless.

The elevator doors part to reveal Teddy's immaculate apartment, which he definitely doesn't clean himself. I don't see him right away, but I hear him walking across the inviting gray hardwood floors. I step off, slide out of my shoes, and set them aside, then pad across the fluffy white area rug and into the kitchen, following the sound of his steps.

There, standing in nothing but a pair of black athletic shorts, is Teddy, pouring coffee into two identical white ceramic mugs.

Even with my side view of him, I can still see the way those shorts are barely hanging on to his trim hips, showing off the shadows of his six-pack and the defined *V* leading down to the one part of him I'm a bit more familiar with than the rest of our friend group. Although they still don't know that. And I'd like to keep it that way. That's just one of the many things we need to discuss today.

"I hope you still drink your coffee black," he mutters, shooting me a sideways glance and a smile. "Because I'm all out of creamer." The muscles in his arms ripple and contract as he sets the coffeepot down, then rakes his fingers through his bed head.

Screw him for not putting on a shirt before I got here. I've already spent plenty of my day distracted by him and this sex-tape situation. Now I have to try not to stare at his abs too? I weigh the option of asking him to put on a shirt, but that would mean acknowledging the fact that I noticed how damn good he looks. So I guess it's time to implement a little self-control.

"Black coffee is great." I sigh, locking my gaze on the top of his head. "I just need something to keep me alert while we discuss your case."

He hands me my mug, then grabs his own before taking a seat on a bar stool. "So you're saying you'll be my attorney?"

I nod, perching on the stool next to him as I let the coffee hit my lips. It's strong. And so am I, for keeping my eyes level with Teddy's. "Yes, I'll be your attorney. But I have a few conditions. The first of which is a promise from you that you'll keep quiet about this."

He narrows his emerald eyes at me. "What do you mean?"

"I mean I don't want our friends, or anyone else for that matter, to know any details about this situation. I just had brunch with Bailey, and it was a battle not to tell her. But I think it's better if we handle this ourselves without having to answer millions of questions from our friends."

"Shit." Teddy looks down into his coffee mug, shifting uncomfortably in his seat. "It's kind of too late for that."

Oh shit. My stomach tightens as a combination of worry and anger builds inside me. "Oh my God, TK. Did you already tell the guys?"

"God, no, I'm not that dumb," he says. "The guys don't know a thing. They would never let me hear the end of it. But I did tell someone. The head of PR for the team."

The knot in my stomach loosens a bit. "Oh. Okay," I whisper, steadying my breath. "That's not quite as bad."

"It seemed stupid not to. It's literally her job to deal with shit like this. And this has got to be one of the worst public relations nightmares in the history of the Ice Hawks franchise. Or at least it will be, if that tape gets out."

"The tape won't get out," I snap. "It can't. We'll both be ruined if it does. Which is another reason why I didn't want you telling anyone." I can feel my grip on my mug getting tighter and tighter, so I set my coffee down. Maybe I need to lay off the caffeine a bit.

"It's gonna be okay. Breathe for me." Teddy puts a reassuring hand on my shoulder, and I feel the tension instantly drain from my body. He still has a calming effect on me, even after all these years. "I didn't tell her it was you in the video. But I did tell her I wanted to hire you as my lawyer. I was firm in that, even though she seemed to think I should use the team lawyer."

My lips tighten into a frown as I think his words over. "She might be right. The team lawyer knows the Ice Hawks' legal guidelines inside and out. And there's something to be said for a lawyer who can be more objective. Someone who isn't . . . *personally involved* in the matter."

"No way." Teddy shakes his head. "I don't want to use the team lawyer. That guy doesn't give a shit about me the way you do. I know you've got my back. And you've got skin in the game." He pauses, a smirk tugging at his lips. "Literally."

I shrug his hand off my shoulder and fold my arms across my chest. "I thought you said you'd knock off that sexual innuendo stuff."

He sets his coffee on the counter, putting his hands up in front of him in surrender. “Look, I’m trying here. The point is, I know how driven you are. And there isn’t another lawyer in the goddamn world who wants this scandal buried more than you do.”

I chew nervously on my lower lip. “You’re right about that.” With one last deep breath, I hold out my hand and he slaps his into it, giving me a firm handshake.

“So, what now?” he asks, looking at me with expectant eyes.

“Well, first,” I smirk, “how about you let go of my hand and show me this email?”

He gives my hand a gentle squeeze before releasing it, and then lifts his mug to his lips.

Oh God . . . I hope we can do this.

No, there can’t be any hoping.

We have no other options. We must get this done.

CHAPTER FOUR

Crossing T's and Dotting I's

Sara

It's seven a.m. on Monday morning, and the smell of printer ink and stale coffee is like a warm welcome back. Well, for me at least.

I know most people can't wait to leave work at the end of the day, but there's something about the Carroll and Associates office that feels like a second home to me. Maybe it's because I've been working here since I was an intern before my senior year of college. The fact that I spend more time here than I do at my own apartment may also be to blame. Whatever the reason, the buzz of the paralegals making copies and the legal associates clicking their red pens is soothing to me. It's a reminder that, unlike at my apartment, I'm not alone.

"Good morning, Sara." David Carroll, the managing partner of the firm, gives me a slight wave as I walk by his office. David has spent the last thirty years building his reputation as the best defense attorney in the city. My first summer interning for him, I was shaking in my heels out of sheer intimidation. But after I graduated law school at the top of my class, he immediately reached out with a job offer. Since then, I've considered him a mentor and a friend.

"Good morning, David. Happy Monday."

I return his wave but quickly move along to the break room for a cup of coffee. He's too busy for office chitchat, and I've got a full caseload too. Especially now that I've agreed to take on one more client, one I have a personal interest in.

Once I settle into my own office, I boot up my computer and review my case files, determining what needs my attention first. While I know I should be practical and address some of my cases with harder deadlines, I know I won't be able to get any other work done until I tend to the one client I can't get off my mind—Teddy.

I pull up the email Teddy forwarded me and read it over to refresh my memory of the details of this threat. The hacker didn't mention anything about money in the email, but I know it'll be brought up the second we respond. No doubt about it. Any weirdo behind a keyboard trying to ruin somebody's life has got to be in it for a profit.

I take a deep breath, roll my shoulders back, and crack my knuckles. All right, Sara. Time to write a cease-and-desist letter. Something I've done a hundred times before.

Just because my ass is on the line—my bare ass, literally on camera, in this case—doesn't mean this process is any different. It takes a few rounds of edits to craft something that perfectly balances the legal jargon with an underlying sense of "don't mess with me, I mean business," but the final product is something I'm proud to hit SEND on.

Once the letter is sent, I pull up the firm's list of go-to private investigators and draft an inquiry email to the first name on the list. A cease-and-desist letter will hold this anonymous creep legally accountable, but it won't make him drop everything and forget the whole thing ever happened. If we really want to keep this video from getting out, we have to find this guy and hold him to every letter of the laws he's breaking.

The PI responds to my email right away, giving me a recap of his impressive background in cyber security. *Perfect.* He's hired. This creepazoid hacker is going the fuck down.

Okay, cease and desist? Check. Private investigator? Check. What's next?

Normally, this is the part of the process where I would draft an extensive email to the client, informing them of where we stand on all matters. But this is Teddy. I'm not even sure he'd be able to process half the legal jargon I would throw his way in a professional email. I'd better just give him a call.

I shut my office door, then tap Teddy's contact on my phone screen. He picks up on the first ring.

"Did we catch him?"

I roll my eyes. What does Teddy think lawyers do for a living? Chase down bad guys like dog-catchers from old cartoons?

"No, Teddy. We didn't catch him. It's a little soon for that. But I sent a cease-and-desist letter, which basically means this creep knows you've got legal representation and we want him to knock it off."

The line is silent for a long moment, and when Teddy finally says something, he sounds annoyed. "Does that even do anything? Of course he knows I want him to knock it off. Or her. Whatever. When do we get to the real stuff?"

I have to physically bite my tongue to keep from snapping at him. "Teddy, I'm in the process of hiring a private investigator. It's only been two days, and there are a lot of t's to cross and i's to dot. Just know that we're doing all the right things to stop the world from seeing this video. I promise. I want this stopped as much as you, so don't think that I won't be working my ass off to make sure it's never seen by anyone other than us, and the creep who's got his hands on it."

A queasy feeling tugs at my gut, reminding me that if Teddy had kept his promise all those years ago and deleted the video like he said he would, we wouldn't have to stop *anyone* from seeing this video. But unfortunately, that's not the reality we're living in. And living in a fantasyland of what-ifs isn't going to stop our sex tape from going viral.

"All right, I'm sorry," he says. "I'm just anxious about it. I was shit today at practice. It was like I'd never worn a fucking pair of skates before. I can't seem to focus on anything but this."

Although Teddy can't see me, I nod in agreement. "Trust me, you're not the only one who is super distracted by this. But I'm doing everything I can. What you can do in the meantime is put some money on retainer for my services. I can have my assistant email you the details."

"Got it. I can do that."

A lump forms in my throat at the determination in his voice. I know he wants to do more to help, but there's really nothing he can do. "I need to go. I have other cases that need my time."

"Of course, Sara." His tone is suddenly calm and sincere. "Seriously, thank you for this. Thank you for everything. I know I'm freaking out, but I couldn't do this without you."

The sweetness in his voice sends a familiar tingle dancing up my spine. I remember that tingle. I used to get it all the time when Teddy and I studied together. I haven't felt it since.

"You're welcome, TK. Let's touch base tomorrow."

After we hang up, I set my phone to DO NOT DISTURB and slip it into my purse. Now that I've got that out of the way, I need to seriously focus. I've got a case set to go to trial in a few weeks, and an endless amount of preparation work I need to get done.

I spend the rest of my day buried in that case,

drafting memos and email correspondence with the client until I can't feel my fingers anymore. It's a miracle I don't have carpal tunnel yet with the percentage of my day I spend typing.

As the room turns a bit colder, a sign that the sun is setting behind the Seattle skyline, there's a knock on my office door. I must have forgotten to open it again after my call with Teddy earlier.

"Come in!" I call, and in walks David, carrying his briefcase in one hand and pushing his tortoiseshell glasses up the bridge of his nose with the other.

"Working hard?" he asks, one eyebrow raised. "You haven't left your office all day. I was starting to think you must have fallen asleep in here."

I laugh, shaking my head. "The opposite, actually. I haven't had a moment of downtime all day."

"Well, a few of the partners and I are going to grab a drink to celebrate that O'Bannon case finally wrapping up. I wanted to extend that invitation to you."

My heart leaps in my chest. An associate being invited to happy hour with the partners is practically unheard of. Turning down this invite isn't even an option.

“I wouldn’t miss it.” I smile, turning my computer off for the night. There will always be work to get done, but an invite to a partners-only happy hour is a rare opportunity.

The cocktail lounge down the street from our office is packed as usual with people from all sectors of corporate America, each of them trying to take the edge off the workday. David leads me to the back, where the other partners are already gathered at a table, most of them sipping dark liquor.

“Sara Dawson.” One of my colleagues clucks his tongue, his eyes lighting up with surprise. “I don’t think I saw you all day. Did you get trapped underneath a stack of case files?”

My lips form a tight smile. “Maybe not physically, but definitely metaphorically.”

Everyone at the table laughs in response, and any anxiety I had about this happy hour dissolves as I slide into one of the open seats. These men have become like family to me over the years. They want to see me succeed. And someday, in the not so distant future, I won’t be the only odd woman out at this table.

Well, I’ll still be the only woman. But I won’t be an associate anymore. I’ll be a partner.

Normally, thinking about being the first female partner of the firm makes me over-the-moon happy. So, why is there an insane tightness in my chest all of a sudden?

It takes me a second before it clicks.

Oh, that's right. There's still the matter of a certain career-ruining video that could stand in my way.

I've been steadily climbing the ladder to partner for the last few years. But if that video surfaces, I have a feeling the ladder will be knocked down underneath me before I can catch my grip.

The first female partner at a top firm being tied to a sex tape? Never in a million years. I'd be surprised if I could ever work in law again after that. And then what? All the years of late nights in the office and going home to lonely microwave dinners for one would be for nothing. I would have wasted the best years of my life chasing something, only to have it all snatched away from me. Just because of one stupid decision I made when I was twenty.

"What can I order for you, Sara?" David asks. "The firm is paying tonight."

"Actually, I think I need to head out." I shift awkwardly out of my seat, feeling the color draining from my face. "I just remembered there's a client who was expecting a call from me today who I forgot to touch base with." I note the disappointment in David's eyes, so I offer a bit of damage control. "The client always comes first. That was one of the first things you said to me when I interned for you, remember?"

David's look of disappointment fades into a proud smile. "Of course, how could I forget? I admire your work ethic, Sara. That's exactly what I look for in a potential partner."

"I always do my best," I squeak in the most chipper voice I can muster.

But when it comes to stopping whoever is behind this anonymous email, I don't know if my best will be good enough.

CHAPTER FIVE

Pink Is My New Favorite Color

Teddy

Damn.

That's my first thought when I spot Sara stepping off the elevator and into the wide marble hallway of the Ice Hawks' headquarters. She's dressed in a black pencil skirt and a cream-colored silk blouse that fits perfectly over her curves, and her dark hair falls in neat waves to the top of her shoulders. But it's her lips that leave me feeling a little weak. They're painted a bright berry-pink color, and *holy shit*, do I want to kiss her right now.

What the hell is wrong with me? Reel it in, dude.

Those gorgeous full lips lift in a polite smile when she gets close. "Teddy," she murmurs, tipping her head. "Sorry I'm late."

I glance down at my watch. "You're not."

She huffs out a sigh, waving her hand. "By two minutes. But parking was hell."

"Yeah, sorry about that. I should have warned you. It's the lunchtime rush from all the nearby offices."

She nods. "Shall we do this thing?"

I swallow, fighting to regain my composure, and usher her toward the conference room at the far end of the hall where the meeting awaits. Her black heels click along beside me, and I steal another quick glance at her.

When we enter the small conference room with its glass table and six leather chairs, LaShonda stands and offers her hand to Sara.

"LaShonda Brown, head of public relations for the Ice Hawks." Her smile is guarded, even if her demeanor is friendly.

"Sara Dawson of Carroll and Associates. It's very nice to meet you."

LaShonda nods as we take our seats. "I wish it were under better circumstances, but yes."

When I first went to the head of PR, I was nervous and more than a little hesitant to come clean about the crisis I was facing. But from the first words out of LaShonda's mouth, I knew I'd done the right thing. She's tough and smart, and I truly believe her number one goal is looking out for the players. Plus, I haven't received a nasty phone call from the coach or GM, so I believe she's held up her end of the bargain not to tell anyone—at least not yet—and now we just need to convince her to keep it that way.

"I trust that Teddy brought you up to speed on what he's facing?" Sara asks.

"I'll be honest with you here, Sara." LaShonda leans forward and folds her hands on the table in front of her. "I advised Mr. King that it would be better to have one of the team's lawyers handle this."

Sara nods. "I'm aware of that. And I think that was very astute of you. But I can assure you, I'm fully prepared to do whatever it takes to get the best possible outcome in this case."

I steal another glance in Sara's direction and find it hard to look away. She's not intimidated in the slightest, even though this woman just told her, essentially, she doesn't want her here.

And, *Jesus*, that lipstick. That goddamn pink lipstick—it's killing me. If I kissed her, I'd get it all over me. So, why does the idea of that excite me so much?

LaShonda turns toward me, frowning. "Teddy, I'm going to be blunt here. I've kept this quiet because you asked me to, and I respect you. I know you want to handle this with your own attorney, but I can't advise that. We need to loop in the team's lawyers and team management. We need to—"

"I'm the other person in the video," Sara says, her voice stern.

LaShonda's gaze swings to Sara and her lips part. She looks as surprised as I feel.

Sara didn't want anyone else knowing. There's no reason for her to out herself—except for the fact she's obviously fighting hard to take on this case. Fighting hard for me.

LaShonda clears her throat. "You're . . ." She looks between us, studying us as though she's working out the details of our past escapade in her head.

Yeah, lady. It happened. Sorry, not sorry.

Sara nods. "Yes. So you can see why I'd have

a vested interest in ensuring this video never gets released. Not some overpaid team attorney who punches in at eight and is gone by five. This is my *life*."

I give Sara a sympathetic look, but she doesn't meet my eyes.

LaShonda taps her pen on the edge of the table, still thinking. "Well, that certainly does change things. I'm willing to work with you here, willing to play by your rules, if you'll do something for me. Something that I think will help."

I lean closer. "What's that?"

LaShonda chooses her next words carefully, straightening her shoulders. "Revenge porn is a thing, Teddy, and whoever has it out for you now has this video as leverage. I'm sorry to tell you that it will most likely get out one way or another. The publicist in me wants to spin this."

Spin it how?

"Just say it," I tell her, my stomach suddenly filling with nervous energy. "Sara can be my lawyer if we agree to . . . what?"

"You two agree to start dating, to pretend to be in a committed relationship for the sake of the media. And that way, if and *when* this thing does get out, you're not some wild, reckless playboy filming hookups, which would probably result in your sponsorships drying up faster than you can slap a puck into a net. Instead, you're in a committed, mature relationship with a woman, and some creep released a video of you two. It makes for a much better spin, what with your privacy being violated and all that."

"My privacy has been violated," I say sternly.

LaShonda holds up her hands. "I know that. I'm just giving you my honest opinion here. This would create the least amount of stir amongst your sponsors, your team, and the public."

And probably piss off my coach less. She's right. *Shit, this is crazy.*

"I'll do it," I say firmly. Sara has gone pale beside me, and I reach over and give her hand a squeeze. "Sara?"

"I—I'll think about it. I need to get back to the office. Excuse me." She stands and rushes for the door.

What the hell?

Grabbing her briefcase from the floor, I follow

her into the hall and lightly grip her elbow to stop her from trying to flee. "Wait."

Sara spins around to face me. She's still pale, but her blue eyes are bright as they blaze on mine. "Thanks." She takes the briefcase from my hands and holds it in front of her like a shield.

"Say something. Please."

She swallows, those distracting pink lips pressing together in a line as she does. "This is crazy."

"So? We can handle a little crazy, can't we?"

She inhales deeply and lets it out slowly. "I really do have another meeting to get to."

I nod. "Think about it. That's all I'm asking."

"I will."

Taking a step back, I shove both hands into my pockets. "I'll call you later. We can work out the details."

Without so much as a nod, Sara turns again, this time for the elevators, and rushes off.

Is the idea of fake-dating me really that awful?

• • •

"You have any bread?" I ask, riffling through my grandfather's fridge. I pull out a package of lunch meat and give it a sniff. Seems all right.

"I think so," he says. "Third cupboard over." He watches while I locate the loaf of bread and make myself a quick sandwich. "You're going to ruin your dinner."

I laugh. Twenty-eight years old, and he still treats me like a little kid.

I hopped on a flight to Denver this afternoon to spend the evening with my grandpa Joe. I don't see him nearly enough anymore, and that weighs on me, especially since he got diagnosed with dementia a few months ago. Grandpa Joe is the one who stepped up and raised me when my parents were struck and killed by a drunk driver when I was four years old, so there's nothing I won't do for him.

"I won't," I say. "I'm starving, and I want to go fix the mailbox before it gets dark. It's leaning pretty bad."

He nods. "Yeah, it's been like that for a month. Bad windstorm did that."

A month? I'm surprised they're still delivering his mail into the thing and not making him drive to the post office to retrieve it. The box has nearly fallen over.

"I'll get it straightened out, and then I'll make us dinner. Cool?"

"Whatever you say." He nods.

I'll barely be here for twenty-four hours, but it'll be just enough time to do a couple of chores for him around the house and drive him to his doctor's appointment in the morning. Maybe I can take him out to his favorite diner for pancakes before I have to head back to the airport.

My desire for more time with him is driving all my decision-making lately. I'm starting to recognize the fact that he won't be around forever.

And as a free agent, I'm not committed to Seattle next year. I've heard that Denver is looking at me for a possible trade. Moving to the Colorado team would mean I'd be closer to my grandpa and could watch over him and take care of him more easily. Of course, Grandpa Joe is resistant to this plan, mostly because he doesn't want to inconvenience me.

How could it be an inconvenience to look after the man who set aside his entire retirement to raise a four-year-old? And he didn't just look after me, but made sure I had the best of everything. He got a part-time job at the factory in town to pay for my hockey equipment when I showed an interest, and drove me to five a.m. ice time six days a week. When I was twelve, he let me join the travel league and went with me to every away game. He went above and beyond, and I should too. Anyway, it weighs on me a lot.

I finish my sandwich while Grandpa flips through that morning's newspaper. I didn't even know they still print the damn things. It's obvious he already read it this morning—the pages are crinkled and there's a coffee stain on one edge.

"I'm going to go fix your mailbox. Tools still in the garage?" I ask, standing and placing my plate in the sink.

He nods, rising too. "I'll keep you company."

That night, after the mailbox was fixed, a hornets' nest removed from his back porch, and steaks were grilled and eaten, Grandpa fell asleep in his recliner in the living room. I helped him to bed and then turned off the documentary we were watching on honeybees. Fascinating little things. I couldn't help but draw a comparison between their queen and Sara—she was tough as nails in today's meetings, even if she did get spooked at the end.

Now I've stripped down to a pair of boxers and am lying in bed across the hall. It's dark except for the glow of my phone. I told Sara I'd call her later, but I opt for a text, since I'm not sure if my voice carrying across the hall would wake my grandfather.

I shoot off a message to her. `Hey, babe.`

`Babe??`

I chuckle and keep typing. `Yeah. We're practically dating now. Didn't you hear?`

I smile to myself at that last remark, but it fades as soon as my phone starts ringing.

She's calling me.

"Hey," I whisper.

"Hey." For a second I think she's about to rip into me for calling her *babe*, just like she did about the sexual innuendos I made in my apartment. "Where are you? Why are you whispering?"

"I'm in Denver."

She pauses for a minute. "But there's not a

game tonight. And the day after tomorrow, you're playing here."

I didn't know she follows my schedule that closely. Then again, most of Seattle does, so maybe I shouldn't read anything into it.

I shift on the narrow bed, propping another pillow under my head. "I came here to check on my grandpa. He's asleep across the hall."

She makes a humming sound. "I forgot, you grew up there, didn't you?"

"Yeah. Well, mostly. I moved here after my parents died. I was born in Wisconsin."

It's not a piece of information I've given her before, and Sara takes her time processing it. She knows I was raised by my grandfather, but I've never told her the reason why.

"How old were you?"

"Little. I was four."

"God, I'm sorry. What the hell is wrong with me? Here you are facing one horrible situation, and now I'm probing you with questions on something even worse. I'm sorry. Let's change the subject."

"No, it's okay. Honestly, I'm happy you called."

"You are?" she asks, her voice lifting.

"Yeah. You distract me."

"In a good way?"

"In a good way." My thoughts flash to earlier—to that pink lipstick that I wanted to mess up, that I wouldn't have minded getting all over me—and my breath quickens.

The line goes quiet for a moment, and I wonder if she's thinking about what LaShonda said earlier like I am.

"So, are you going to fake-date me or what?"

Sara chuckles, and I can picture her smile. "I don't know. Are you going to be a good fake boyfriend?"

"Oh, I'm the best there is."

She laughs again. "Let's talk about it when you get back, okay?"

"Yes, dear," I murmur.

After we say good night, I lie awake for a long time thinking about Sara, and then about my grandpa. I'm normally a pretty easygoing guy and not much gets me stressed, but this situation with his health does. I just wish there was an easy answer, and there's not. It's so hard watching the person you love most in this world slowly fade away, which I fear is exactly what's going to happen. At least Sara distracted me for a bit.

Man, my life has turned into a shit show. Let's hope it gets better before it gets worse.

CHAPTER SIX

Missed Opportunities

Teddy

"Hey, dumbass! I'm open."

Asher glares at me, banging his stick repeatedly on the ice to catch my attention. I fling the puck his way but it goes wide, and he lets out an unhappy grunt as it whizzes past him, straight into the corner.

We're playing a scrimmage game, and my focus has been absolute shit today. I can't complete a pass to save my life. I haven't even scored once yet, which is saying something, because the only thing standing between me and that net is our rookie backup goalie, Morgan. He's good, but he's nowhere near as solid as Owen. I should have a couple on net by now. Asher definitely would have sank one in if I'd fed it to him in time.

I try to tell myself I'm off my game because of the quick midweek travel I did to Denver, but I know that's not it. If I'm being honest, I'm still bothered by how quickly Sara shot down the idea of pretending to date me like it was the worst thing in the world. It stings more than it should.

When the scrimmage finally ends, I hobble down the tunnel toward the dressing room and strip out of my skates, jersey, and pads. After a quick shower, I find Owen, Justin, and Asher in the dressing room discussing something in hushed tones. I quickly dress and slip my feet into my tennis shoes before joining their huddle.

"What's up?" I ask, more than a little curious about what has them whispering. If we're plotting more hazing on the rookies, then I totally want in on that action.

Owen has a huge smile on his face. Justin gives him a playful shove, which only makes Owen grin wider.

"Will someone please tell me what the hell is going on here?"

Justin clears his throat. "Owen is going to propose to Becca."

My stomach tightens as my eyes flash to Owen's. "Whoa. That's huge, man. Congratulations."

"She hasn't said yes yet. Better not jinx me." He reaches out to return my handshake.

"She'll say yes," Asher says, rolling his eyes. "You two are like *disgustingly* in love."

"Did you buy the ring yet?" Justin asks.

Owen gives him a sheepish nod. He turns and reaches into his backpack, producing a small black box, and when he opens it, we all stagger a step back.

Holy crap, that is one big rock.

"Damn." Justin hisses low under his breath.

Proudly, Owen rattles off something about clarity and facets. When I hear the terms *flawless* and *four carats*, that's all I need to know to understand that this ring costs much more than most people make in a year. It's absolutely stunning.

The perfect piece of jewelry he's holding is a reminder of how far I am away from giving a woman something like that. First, I'd need to get someone to agree to date me, and seeing as one of my good friends doesn't even want to fake-date me, I'm thinking it's way off. That can't possibly bode well for my chances of finding lasting love.

"Congratulations, man. You two are perfect together," I say, giving him my nod of approval.

Becca is the best thing to ever happen to Owen. He was a manwhore of the highest order before she tamed him. I'm still not sure how she did that, entirely, but it's obvious he's crazy about her.

Justin thumps Owen on the back in a bro hug, while Asher shoves his hands into his pockets. Once the ring has been safely tucked away again, we start for the exit.

"Hey, what's going on with Denver?" Asher asks, bumping my shoulder with his. "Aren't they looking at you?"

I nod. "Yeah, they're looking, but I don't know anything yet. As far as I'm concerned, this is my team. And until that changes, my mind-set is still one-hundred percent here."

And it's the truth. Just because I'm a free agent and could be offered a contract somewhere else doesn't mean I can allow my focus to start drifting now. I have games to play and win, and until someone comes through with a contract, I need to keep my head down and focus.

Asher nods. "Fair enough."

We part ways in the parking lot, and as I drive away, I spot Owen's face in my rearview mirror. He's still smiling like he won the freaking lottery.

Man, what I wouldn't give for a little bit of that feeling right about now. These last few days, all my concentration has been jacked, and I can't help the nagging feeling inside me that something is missing.

By the time I make it home to my empty apartment, I realize what that something is.

Justin and Owen are both in serious relationships—Owen's going to be engaged soon, for God's sake—and I'm alone. And I guess it's hitting me for the first time how different my life is from theirs. Sure, Asher is single too, but it doesn't seem to bother him. He's with a different girl every weekend.

Sliding my keys onto the counter, I pull open the fridge and grab a bottle of water.

One of the biggest decisions of my career is coming up, and I have no one to talk it over with. No one to talk to about my grandpa's failing health, or about the possible trade to Denver, or about how some weirdo is threatening to release a sex tape of me. Just a quiet, empty apartment. It's never bothered me before, and I have no idea why it's starting to now.

Leaning one hip against the kitchen counter, I sort through the mail my housekeeper left for me. A thick silver envelope catches my attention, and I groan when I realize what it is. Ripping open the foil paper, I slide out a card-stock invitation and scan the overly formal script letters.

Mr. & Mrs. Stuart Jamison request the honor of your presence . . .

Groaning, I shove a hand through my damp hair. I can't believe my ex actually went through with it.

I got a save-the-date card in the mail a few months ago, and I thought, *She's not actually going to invite me to her engagement party, is she?* But the card in my hand proves otherwise. The engagement party is this weekend at one of the nicest restaurants downtown.

Can't I just send a gift or something? Does a toaster say, Hey, we used to bone before you decided it wasn't my dick you wanted to be your for-

ever dick?

Obviously, Kelly and I were close at one time, but this is awkward. Why the hell did she invite me? It's then I realize this was probably her father's idea—he was always wanting to talk hockey with me and seemed intrigued by the idea of me being a pro player.

Tossing the envelope back onto the counter, I grab my phone and make my way into my living room, sinking down onto the couch. There might be one bright side to getting invited to this engagement party.

I pull up Sara's name on my phone and bite my lower lip. *Here goes nothing . . .*

CHAPTER SEVEN

Drunk Words and Sober Thoughts

Sara

I have somewhat of a track record of being taken on weird dates. It's happened a lot over the years. Between boring documentary showings, awkward improv comedy classes, and once, an honest-to-God rodeo, I've always been the type to have a story that begins with "You won't believe what I did this weekend." Of course, that all changed when I committed to making partner and my dating life went out the window. For the past few years, my weekends have been, well, believable.

Until today.

I can confidently say that, on the weirdness scale, accompanying Teddy to his ex's engagement party is above and beyond any other date I've been on. The bonus weirdness comes from the fact that it's not even a real date. It's nothing more than an opportunity to start making our phony relationship public. But even if this relationship is fake, the giddy, jittery feeling that's been fluttering in my stomach all day is very, very real.

As I perch on a stool near my bathroom sink with my curling wand in hand, I review the answers Teddy and I prepped to any potential questions that may arise, like how long we've been together, when we met, all the good stuff people ask new couples. We've gone over everything we can think of to make tonight run smoothly. I even bought a brand-new little black dress that almost makes me feel hot enough to be dating a professional hockey player. So I have no reason to be nervous. But I am.

And then, as I hold my breath to lock my waves down with hairspray, I suddenly remember something one of my professors told me in law school before I took the bar exam. Something about nervousness and excitement being practically the same emotion. They both make your heart beat faster and give you that jittery feeling in your stomach.

Maybe I'm not nervous for my date. Maybe I'm excited for it.

And who could blame me? All of the stress and legal gymnastics of trying to keep this sex tape under wraps has put a lot of pressure on Teddy and me. A night of taking advantage of an open bar doesn't sound so bad. Plus, I haven't been on a date since half past forever, and even though it is a fake one, Teddy and I always have a good time together. Granted, we mostly hang out in group settings these days, but back in college, when it was just us two, he used to make me laugh like no one else could.

"One shot or two?"

My memory rewinds to a twenty-one-year-old Teddy sitting on the floor of my dorm junior year, mixing us vodka lemonades. My RA was dating one of the older guys on the hockey team and never busted us for drinking in the dorm.

"Two," I said, holding up two fingers like a peace sign as he measured the shots and poured them into my red plastic cup full of lemonade.

"Oh, sure, you give me the peace sign now," he teased, giving my oversize sorority shirt a flirty tug. "But a few more of those things, and we both know you're gonna be anything but peaceful."

I held my hand up to my face to keep lemonade from coming out my nose. "Are you saying I'm a loud drunk?"

A smirk tugged at his full lips as he cupped my chin in his calloused hand, leaning in until I could smell the potent liquor on his breath. "Not a loud drunk. A fun drunk. But not as fun as you are in bed," he teased before capturing my lips with his, coaxing my tongue into his mouth in one hot, vodka-fueled kiss after another.

The hairspray fumes pull me out of my trip down memory lane.

I have to keep getting ready, but the warm buzz of the memory stays firmly cemented in my heart. That's precisely the sort of feeling I need to call on to make this fake relationship convincing.

Teddy gave me some of my best memories that year. He also gave me a record number of orgasms. If I can harness the power of those two simple facts, I'm positive I can fool a bunch of strangers into thinking I'm head over heels for Teddy King.

Once I slip into my new strappy black dress and my black chunky heels to match, I feel absolutely unstoppable. Forget pantsuits. If I could wear this in the courtroom, I wouldn't lose a single case.

Watching myself in my full-length mirror, I pivot a few times to ensure I'm looking good from all angles, then add a swipe of deep red lipstick to complete the look. *Perfect.* And just in time too. My phone buzzes on the vanity with a text from my hot date.

Hey, babe, I'm parked out front. Ready to make our acting debut?

I grab my purse with one hand and my phone with the other to send him a quick reply.

As ready as I'll ever be. Be down in a sec.

Outside my apartment, Teddy's car is about as easy to spot as a diamond in a bowl of oatmeal. Among the used SUVs and modest sedans parked on my street, there's one sleek black Mercedes with tinted windows that immediately sticks out. I may not be able to see through the tinting, but I'm willing to bet any amount of money that I know exactly who is behind the wheel.

I tug open the passenger's door, and sure enough, there's Teddy, one wrist draped lazily over the wheel. His dark hair is neatly combed back, and he's wearing a crisp black suit that perfectly frames the breadth of his muscular shoulders. It looks like it was made for him, and knowing Teddy, it probably was.

When he turns to meet my gaze, I spot a flash of crimson from beneath his jacket. A red tie, nearly the exact shade of my lipstick. We almost match too well.

“Goddamn, Sara.” He hisses under his breath as his eyes trace the curves of my hips. “You look incredible. If your goal was to upstage the bride-to-be, mission accomplished.”

His tone holds a hint of wonder, and a hot shiver runs down my arms. His gaze is still fixed on my curves. It’s been a long time since a man has taken me in like this, and it feels surprisingly good. Almost too good to be fake.

“Is this dress okay?” I ask sheepishly. “Should I go change into something less—”

Teddy shakes his head, gesturing for me to get in the car. “Not a chance. You look like the fake girlfriend of my dreams. Let’s roll.”

With a low purr of the powerful engine, Teddy pulls into traffic.

“So, how long did you and Kelly date?” I ask, glancing down at the invitation that’s been placed on top of the cupholders. It has the address to a swanky restaurant downtown I’ve never been to, but always wanted to try.

"Uh, two years?" he says, his eyes on the road.

"Was it serious?"

"For me, yes."

"Interesting," I say, more to myself than to him.

But Teddy just shrugs. "When I go in, I go all in."

I guess that's true of him. It's especially true with hockey. The man has made it into a stellar career for himself.

"So, what happened? Is there going to be any drama tonight?"

He shakes his head. "None at all. It's been years since we broke up. I think her dad liked me more than she did. I'm pretty sure that's the only reason I got the invite."

The restaurant isn't too far from my apartment, allowing us only a few precious minutes to review the details of our half-fake, half-true backstory one last time. I feel like I'm preparing a client for court as I run through the questions one by one, letting Teddy rehearse his answers. Luckily, he doesn't seem as on edge about this as I am. His voice is cool and smooth, like a shot of tequila, as he runs through the answers we agreed on.

"How'd I do?" he asks as he turns the car into a parking spot and cuts the ignition.

We're here already? Those ten minutes flew by in what felt like seconds, and I suddenly realize that I didn't pay attention to a single word Teddy said. I've been too focused on the five o'clock shadow creeping down his chiseled jaw. I hate to admit it, but it's sexy as hell.

"You did great," I say, not wanting to admit that I've been too busy ogling him to listen. Whether he did well or not, it doesn't matter. It's time for us to take the stage.

When Teddy steps out of the car, allowing me my first full view of him tonight, my breath stills in my chest.

Holy fuck. I thought he looked handsome the night of the auction, but I guess "looking good for charity" Teddy has nothing on "looking hot to make sure my ex knows what she missed out on" Teddy. He saunters over to me, adjusting his cuff links and giving me an encouraging half smile.

"Should we hold hands?" I offer shyly. "You know, so we look convincing?"

"Great idea." He nods, weaving his strong, thick fingers through mine.

The hairs on my arm stand up in response, and I have to remind myself for what won't be the first or last time tonight that this is all just for show. I still can't believe I agreed to this, but I was a desperate woman who would do anything to keep this tape locked away forever. Plus, what's the harm in spending some time with Teddy?

Inside, the restaurant has been completely rented out for the engagement party. Dozens of guests flit about, snagging hors d'oeuvres from waiters' trays. I had no idea this was going to be such a large event, but I guess if the bride-to-be's ex-boyfriend was invited, it must have been a pretty extensive guest list.

We're hardly two steps into the restaurant when someone calls out for Teddy. More specifically, they call out his jersey number. I almost forgot I was here with a bona fide Seattle celebrity.

We make our rounds, chatting with old acquaintances of Teddy's, and to my surprise, it's not half as awkward as I thought it would be. When Teddy introduces me as his girlfriend, the words fall naturally from his lips without hesitation. I shake the hands of the bride and groom, offering them my congratulations, but we hardly exchange introductions before Teddy is whisked off by a few old college buddies, all of them bragging to their wives that they were friends with *the* Teddy King back in the day.

"The life of dating a hockey player," I say, giving the bride-to-be an apologetic smile. "You know how it is."

Over the course of twenty minutes, I'm introduced to more people than I can count, all of whom Teddy assures me I will never see again. Still, I do my best to smile and greet each one with a "Hi, nice to meet you. I'm Teddy's girlfriend." The more I say it, the easier it is. Even better, no one seems to have too many questions about the details of our relationship.

A few of his friends remember me vaguely from college and make some friendly comments about how it's about time the two of us officially got together, but beyond that, Teddy and I aren't really the most popular topic of conversation. His hockey career is.

Everyone we talk to wants to hear about his exciting life on the ice, but I'm surprised when he mostly keeps his answers brief, directing the conversation back to whoever he's catching up with. This is a humbler side of Teddy that I haven't seen before. Then again, we rarely go out just the two of us, into settings like this one. But I've got to say, I do like this side of him. It's intriguing, and I find myself wanting to discover the other sides of him I've never witnessed before.

After plenty of socializing, we eventually settle in at a table with our drinks—a wheat ale for him, a vodka soda with lemon for me. What use is an open bar if you don't take advantage of it?

"I see you haven't outgrown your vodka-and-lemon phase," Teddy teases, giving me a wink as he takes a long sip of his beer.

"What can I say? I find what I like, and I stick to it." The lemon barely conceals the taste of vodka, but as it washes over my tongue, the familiar taste puts my nerves at ease.

"I'm the same way, actually," he says, nodding toward the bottle in his hand. "I've been drinking the same beer for years. And whenever I travel for games, the guys always give me shit for eating at chain restaurants. But if it ain't broke, don't fix it, right? It's a lot easier than trying to figure out where to get a decent burger in a new town every couple of days."

"No way," I say with a laugh. "You're a chain-restaurant junkie too?"

A smile forms behind his beer bottle as he takes a sip. "Hell yeah, I am. The food is solid, and I know I can trust it. Why change a good thing?"

"Exactly! Tell that to my foodie friends. They're always making fun of my odd love for cheesy chain restaurants with those little pictures on the menu . . . but I don't see what's so bad about a little consistency."

"I guess for our next date I'll have to take you to Chili's then."

I give him a grin. "Don't knock Chili's. I'd enjoy myself more there with a plate of chicken wings than at one of those stuffy places where the food is tiny and contains things like foie gras or calves' brains." I shrug. "I'm pretty low-maintenance on the date scale."

He chuckles, then kills the rest of his beer. "I'm grabbing another one. Do you want another vodka soda?"

I nod, gazing at him. "Why not? It's an open bar, after all."

Teddy grins at me. "My kind of girl."

A weird sensation rushes through my chest as I watch him walk away.

Once we have our second drinks in hand, we launch into a full-on discussion of the pros and cons of each chain restaurant, pausing only so that Teddy can pose for the occasional picture with attendees of the party, looking for proof that they partied with a member of the Ice Hawks.

"Doesn't that annoy you?" I ask in a whisper after what has to be the twelfth picture of the night.

Teddy shakes his head. "Nah. It's the least I can do. My grandpa always says that no one is more important than anyone else. So I try to treat fans that way. They're just as important as I am."

"Is this the grandpa you were visiting in Denver?" I ask, interested in finding out more about him.

"Yup. He's the one who raised me. But he's getting up there in years, and he has dementia. So I don't get a ton of advice from him anymore. Most days, I'm just glad he still remembers my name."

"I get it. My parents are in their late sixties. They had me really late. They say I worry about them too much, but . . ." I shrug, then clear my throat and lift my glass in the air in an effort to steer away from this suddenly sad conversation topic. "I propose a toast."

Teddy furrows his brow but lifts his beer in the air. "Okay, a toast. To what?"

I giggle. The alcohol is clearly getting to me. "I don't know. To . . . chain restaurants?"

"To chain restaurants," Teddy says. "And to open bars."

By the time the party is coming to an end, Teddy and I are both certified tipsy. He suggests the diner across the street as a venue for some drunk food and a few cups of coffee to sober up, or take a cab home. Since I can never say no to a plate of french fries, we're sliding into a booth in no time. The waitress must smell the booze on us, because she instantly pours us each a huge mug of coffee.

"Are we that obvious?" I giggle across the table.

Teddy shrugs. "Who cares? Worst-case scenario, she recognizes me and tells people Teddy King was drunk in here on a Friday with his smokin'-hot girlfriend."

I roll my eyes. "Thanks for the compliment, babe."

He stops in mid-sip of coffee, shaking his head. "No, you can't call me *babe*. I call you *babe*. You have to come up with your own nickname for me."

I scrunch my nose, thinking it over. "What about *baby*?"

"No way." He scoffs. "I once was hooking up with this girl who kept calling me *baby* over and over again in bed. Like she didn't know how to say anything else. It was one of the worst hookups I've ever had."

My eyes narrow, giving him a challenging squint over my coffee mug. "Really? *That's* the worst you've ever had? I don't believe that for a second."

"Okay, okay." He leans back in the booth, folding his arms over his chest. "I'll tell you my worst if you tell me yours."

"Deal." I grin.

"You first, though." His full lips seem to be permanently amused.

Ugh. Of course he's making me go first.

Luckily, our waitress reappears, buying me a little more time to think about it as I place my order for a side of fries. Meanwhile, Teddy orders what sounds like half the menu. The only thing worse than an athlete's appetite is an intoxicated athlete's appetite. The dude can seriously eat.

The waitress leaves to put our orders in with the cook, and as soon as she's out of earshot. Teddy leans across the table, narrowing his eyes at me. "C'mon. Worst hookup story. Tell me."

"Fine." I give in on a sigh. "There was a guy in law school. We hooked up two, maybe three times at my place. But then the first time I went back with him to his apartment, it turned out he had a dog. And this dog absolutely would not leave the room while we were trying to, you know, do the deed." I wiggle my eyebrows.

Teddy throws his head back in an uproarious laugh. "C'mon, Dawson. You just have to lock eyes with the dog right away and show your dominance over it. Let him know who's gonna be the one getting petted tonight."

I hold my hand to my mouth to keep myself from spitting coffee all over the table. "Gross, TK!" Once I've swallowed my coffee and gotten my giggles out, I prop my chin in my hands and blink expectantly at him. "Your turn."

"First, I refuse to believe that's your worst story, but all right, fair is fair." He scans the room to make sure no one is listening in, then wags a finger at me. "But all I'm saying is I wouldn't be telling you this if I were completely sober, okay?"

I blink at him again, not saying a word until he spills.

"Okay, so there was this girl, kind of a jersey-chaser type I met when I first started playing for the Ice Hawks. I took her back to my place and she tried to blow me."

I frown. "*Tried* to blow you?"

"Yeah. Tried," he says, his eyes widening. "And by that I mean she just, like, held my dick in her mouth for a few minutes. She didn't even move. She just held it in there. And then after a while, she winks up at me and says, 'Did that get ya?' I didn't know what the fuck to do, so I said, 'Yeah, thanks.'"

This time, there's no holding back. I cough once, sending coffee all across the table until we're both absolutely cracking up, fumbling with the napkin dispenser to get it cleaned up before the waitress sees.

"I didn't even get to the end!" Teddy protests. "The next time I saw her at a bar a few months later, she was full-on making out with a girl. So I guess my dick turned her off of men for good."

I scoff as I press another napkin into the spill. "Teddy, your dick didn't turn her into a lesbian."

"How could you possibly know that?" His voice is serious and his eyes are on mine.

Suddenly, my mind is racing back to junior year again, sitting on my dorm-room floor with Teddy's arms wrapped around my waist as he shifted me into his lap so I could feel the pressure of his bulge pushed against me.

"Not a loud drunk. A fun drunk. But not as fun as you are in bed."

I look up from the spill and my eyes lock with his for a long, quiet moment. We're not in college anymore, but in his emerald eyes, I still see that same man from my dorm room. The one who kissed me and ground his hips against me and brought me to the edge over and over and over.

"It just didn't," I whisper, my voice shaking as I try desperately to steady my breath. "Trust me, Teddy. *I know.*"

CHAPTER EIGHT

Second Chances

Teddy

"Trust me, Teddy. *I know." Sara's voice is soft but sure, and it sends a tingle drifting straight down to my balls.*

Shit. I guess she does know from personal experience.

My heart beats faster, and I can't help but wonder if she still thinks about hooking up with me. Probably not. I mean, it's ancient history, right? But right now, she's looking at me with those gorgeous sky-blue eyes, and I have to wonder.

Damn, that's an arousing thought, and my body responds accordingly. Which is a little inconvenient for me because we're seated in a booth across from each other at a diner exchanging bad hookup stories. Weird, I know. But there's something so freeing about being with her.

At the engagement party tonight, I had to be *on*, the pro athlete everyone expects and wants a piece of. But now, with Sara, I get to be myself, and I didn't realize how nice that actually feels. I don't have to try to entertain her or put on some show.

I know it's petty, believe me, I do. But the lesser evolved parts of my brain couldn't resist the opportunity to make my ex a little jealous—and Sara is the perfect woman to make anyone's ex jealous. She's a successful attorney, wicked smart, driven, and beautiful. I'm not going to lie, a huge kick of satisfaction surged through me when I introduced Sara to my ex and her new fiancé.

Kelly's lips pouted into a frown as she assessed Sara, and her fiancé, Tuck (seriously, who names their kid Tuck?), looked like he'd swallowed his tongue. It was priceless.

All in all, it wasn't a bad night. Sara and I laughed all through the event, and I even remembered to snap a selfie of us and post it to my social media, so LaShonda should be pleased.

A few seconds later, our food is delivered, and

we dig in. While we talk, I can't resist prodding Sara a little more. What can I say? I'm a sucker for her laugh.

"So, there's no way that lame dog story was your worst hookup ever."

She pops another fry into her mouth and nods. "I swear. It was beyond weird."

I concede the point, passing her the ketchup when I see she's running low. "Fine."

"What about you?" She leans forward, grinning. "That BJ story is the worst you've got?"

I shrug. "It sucked."

"Not literally," she says with a chuckle.

"Still such a brat," I mutter, grabbing a napkin and pass her one too. "Okay, hookup horror stories aside, tell me the worst thing someone could do to turn you off in bed."

Call me crazy, but I *really love* this topic we're edging around. Past hookups. And it has everything to do with the fact that she was one of the best I ever had. I have *very* fond memories of our time together—even if it was forever ago. And I secretly hope she does too.

"Let's just say I've developed a no-phone policy during sex."

I squint at her. "Tell me some knucklehead didn't answer the phone in bed."

She shakes her head. "Nope, he was texting during. Talk about a kick to the ego that my naked body rated less exciting than his text thread."

My gaze latches onto hers and narrows. "That's bullshit. I can attest to the fact that your naked body could make a grown man forget his own damn name."

What? She brought up our history when she insisted my dick wouldn't turn a woman off men for good. Can't I bring it up too?

"It's been a while, TK," she says, her voice soft, unsure.

"You're like a fine wine, babe."

She grins at my implication that she's only gotten better with age, which is absolutely true.

I love this—the talking, the flirting, the subtly bringing up our past. The situation in my pants, however, is less than thrilled.

Too fucking bad.

I'm having way too much fun to stop now.

"What about you?" she asks, dragging a soggy fry through her ketchup as though she's disinterested, but I can tell she's into this conversation too. First, there's the quick pulse thrumming in her neck, and second, she's leaning in toward me across the table. "Any turnoffs?"

A million thoughts flash through my brain at once. I have a lot of turnoffs, actually. Crying after sex is an obvious one. That's not exactly a turn-on. Neither is being self-conscious about your body, or refusing to undress completely even after I've assured you I like your body.

Sara was never like that, though. She was confident and assertive in the bedroom, or the *dorm room*, as it were. She never hid from me or acted embarrassed.

"Gagging noises is a weird one," I settle on. "On the one hand, it's kind of a compliment that my dick is big enough to choke you, but I'm always legit concerned I'm about to be thrown up on."

Sara shakes her head, a smile on her lips. "And here I thought you were going to say performing oral sex on a woman or something."

"God, no. I'm *always* down for some pussy eating."

"Oh my God. Gross, TK." She laughs, but it comes out a little breathless.

"Nothing gross about it, sweetheart." I lean forward, placing my elbows on the table. "My theory is you've gotta treat it like a big plate of barbeque ribs. Dig in. Get messy. And expect to be there a while without caring if you're ever going to finish."

"You're doing God's work," she jokes, meeting my eyes with a grin.

"Do unto others."

Sara giggles, crossing her arms in front of her chest.

Don't look at her tits.

"Oh, I've got another one," I say, trying to distract myself from her perfect chest. "There was once this girl I was making out with who spit in my mouth with no warning. I learned that day I don't like having my mouth spit into."

Sara's eyebrows raise briefly, and then her calm expression is back. "Poor, naive TK. She was probably an alien sent from another planet to lay an egg in your throat."

I burst into easy laughter.

This. This right here is what I love about being with this girl.

She catches me off guard, and no part of her is impressed that I'm a hockey player. We're just two people with a shared history, making each other laugh. Even if this is a fake date, it's hands-down one of the best dates I've ever been on.

It seems as though Sara isn't done reminiscing. She gets a faraway look in her eyes as she pushes her plate away, and I get the sense she's still thinking about the past.

"Why didn't I ever do anything fun and reckless, just for me? Like . . . I don't know, get a tattoo, maybe something cute on my lower back?"

"You don't put a bumper sticker on a Mercedes," I say teasingly, my voice low.

She laughs again. "You were the only fun thing I ever did, Teddy. And that video was pretty reckless."

"Yeah, it was, wasn't it?"

"God, what were we thinking?" She makes a

low sound, shaking her head.

"Me? I was thinking with my dick. I have no idea what your excuse was."

"I guess I was thinking with my vagina." Her eyes meet mine, and there's a slight blush to her cheeks.

I chuckle with easy laughter. "God, I've missed this, Sara. Us. Carefree. Laughing. Hanging together."

We spent so many years hiding our past from our friends and pretending this never happened. What were we thinking?

"I missed us too," she says softly.

After we've finished eating and exchanging dirty stories, I settle our tab and decide I'm more than sober enough to drive home.

With my fingertips trailing along her spine, I escort Sara toward the exit with a satisfied feeling bubbling in my chest.

Game-time decision. Do I invite her back to my place or not?

I lean down and whisper near her ear, "Thank you for coming."

She looks up at me with a surprised expression. "I had more fun than I thought I would."

"So, what you're saying is I'm not a bad fake date, after all?"

"You're not so bad for a fake boyfriend." She sighs, a little smile lingering on her lips.

Who am I kidding? Of course I'm going to invite her back to my place.

"Then I've got just the thing to push this date over the top," I say with a grin.

"And what would that be?"

"Peanut butter ice cream. My place. You in?" I'm banking on the fact it's still her favorite, and when I see the smile tugging at her lips, I know I've won.

She doesn't hesitate. "Let's roll."

Something changes during the car ride over. The air grows thicker, hot with unspoken tension, and the minute we reach my apartment, it all comes to a head. Sara has gone totally quiet on me, and I have no idea what she's thinking.

Is she going to flee? Back out on the whole fake-relationship thing we've got going on? What could have taken root in her head from the time we left the diner till now?

"You okay? You went kinda quiet on me, Dawson," I say as we step into my apartment, and I close the door behind us. I left a light on over the kitchen sink, so there's a soft glow to guide us, but it's dim and the apartment is filled with shadows.

For a second, I think she's about to make some smart remark, maybe call me out on my promise of ice cream, but then she nibbles on her lower lip and meets my eyes. "I want to see it."

I don't have to ask what she wants to see, because one look into her eyes and I just know.

The video.

"I don't think that'd be a very good idea."

My reluctance doesn't dissuade her. After slipping off her heels by the door, her long toned legs carry her toward my laptop, which is sitting on the kitchen island.

"It's not on there," I say as she fiddles with it.

"Then show me."

Against all better judgment, I lead her down the hall toward my study, which I use as a home office.

It's where I pay bills and watch sports tape, and the room contains little more than a desk and an office chair. There's a sad faux plant in the corner and a dusty box of tax returns in the closet. But on the computer perched on the desk is the video she's asking to see.

"For the record, I still think this is a bad idea." I pull off my suit jacket and loosen my tie while I wait for her to change her mind.

"I've never seen it," she says, standing beside the desk with her hands on her hips.

It's obvious I'm not going to deter her. When Sara wants something, she goes after it. We're a lot alike that way.

Sinking into the leather armchair in front of the desk, I fire up the computer and locate the file in question. Even the thumbnail image arouses me. There's nothing sexy about it; it's actually an extreme close-up of her thigh. Sara probably can't even tell what it is, but my dick knows what's about to go down and stands at attention, eager to be put in the game.

"Last chance to back out," I murmur, my finger hovering over the mouse.

Sara shifts restlessly beside me, leaning one

manicured hand against the desk as she gives her head a firm shake. "You know I'm not going to back down. Just show me."

Her tone leaves little room for argument, and I'll admit, I'm more than curious about what her reaction will be when she finally sees this video after all these years.

I take a shallow breath and click PLAY, bringing the video up to full-size.

The first few seconds are of us getting situated on my bed. But once we do, the video versions of us are kissing, my hips happily grinding against hers. She's wearing only a pair of white cotton boy shorts and a lime-green bra, and I have on a pair of gray boxer shorts.

I remember the emotions surging through me like it was yesterday—the heart-pounding feeling in my chest, the horny anticipation running through me, the excitement of being on camera, how her soft skin felt against my fingertips—all of it.

Daring a quick glance up at her, I notice that she's flushed and her breathing is little more than shallow pants.

The video version of me slowly peels her panties down her legs and then tosses them over the side of the bed. Her hands shove into the back of my underwear, pulling my ass closer. I help her, pushing my boxers down and out of the way so she can grind her wet center all over me.

God, I remember how good that felt. A warm shudder pulses through me at the thought of how wet and needy she was.

I want to make a comment, maybe ask her if it's like she remembers, or say something, *anything* to lighten this intense mood that's settled around us, but there are no words. This video is the hottest fucking thing I've ever done, and now I'm sitting here with my costar reliving our porno debut. And there's nothing rehearsed or awkward about the way we moved together. Even back then, we were red-hot combustible chemistry, and there was an ease about us being together.

Onscreen Sara makes a pleasure-filled sound, and real-life Sara looks unsteady on her feet. The moment I finally sink inside her on the video, real-life Sara stumbles forward and sinks into my lap.

"You okay?" I rasp, my voice husky.

She swallows and then nods once. "This is . . ."

Intense.

Hot as fuck.

Excruciating.

Inappropriate.

There are so many adjectives flitting through my brain right about now.

Sara makes a move to extricate herself from my lap, but my forearm tightens around her waist, and she settles in against me once again. I'm more than happy to let her use me as a chair, even if I'm certain she can feel the hard ridge in my dress pants pressing against her ass.

On the screen, my hips move faster between her parted thighs and she crosses her ankles behind my back, urging me even closer. She was always that way, enthusiastic in bed, and I loved it.

Heat courses through my veins, and I stifle a groan. *Jesus, this is torture.* The soft weight of her ass in my lap, the scent of her floral perfume . . . I'm not watching the video anymore, I realize. I'm watching her.

My blood floods with awareness—awareness of everything. Her nearness. Our history. This heated moment.

She bites her bottom lip between her teeth, and

when her eyes stray from the screen to mine, I open my mouth to speak.

"I should . . ." Turn off this video. Abort this mission. Take a vow of chastity. Move to Russia. Something.

Only none of those words come out of my mouth.

I'm not sure when I decide to kiss her. I only know that I'm leaning in and then so is she, her eyes sinking closed. Her lips touch mine and the pressure is firm, yet soft at the same time.

Her full lips part and our tongues touch, my heart racing. A small gasp escapes her as she shifts even closer, squirming in my lap.

God, why did I ever think I could resist this woman? Suddenly, abstaining from this for the past seven years seems like the stupidest thing I've ever done. How and why did we resist this?

Oh, right. Because when she came back at the end of that summer, she had a boyfriend, and then by the time she was single again, I was dating someone. Lather, rinse, repeat. That was how things went for a while.

But now we're both single. Very single. And

kissing.

And, *holy shit*, it's the perfect kiss.

It's not too slow, but it's not rushed either. There's just the right amount of tongue, and so much hot friction in my lap that I harden even more.

I feel so many things in this moment. At the top of that list is horny, of course, but there's also elation, and a sense of relief, because this moment has been years in the making and now it's finally here.

Rising from the chair, I lift her with me and her legs cross behind my back, just like they did in the video moments before. Stalking toward my bedroom, I secure her around me with my forearm under her ass, and Sara presses closer, her tongue still tangling with mine in greedy strokes.

I want to ask her if she's okay with this as I place her in the center of my bed, but considering her tongue hasn't left my mouth, I'm going to take that as a *yes*—she's very much okay with moving this party to my bedroom.

My mouth leaves hers only long enough to kiss a hot line down her neck, and then my fingers are fumbling for the zipper on her dress. She helps me as I give it a tug.

A second later, her dress and my shirt hit the floor and we're kissing again, her fingertips touching the grooves in my ab muscles in a slow, teasing exploration.

"Jesus, Teddy," she says in a whisper, admiring me as her hands roam over my chest. "Look at you."

Even though I'd love for her to look and admire and touch me to her heart's content, right now I have bigger goals.

"Take these off," I say, rubbing my thumb over the front of her underwear as her hips shift restlessly on the bed.

She obeys immediately, hooking her fingers into the black lace and drawing them down her hips. And then she's bare, and it's just soft curves and creamy skin, all on display for me.

I rub my hands along her thighs, pressing one last kiss against her lips before kneeling on the bed between her knees.

Her eyes roam my chest, and I almost want to puff it out, prideful lust pulsing through me. I have a nice chest and have been told so many times, but her eyes don't stop there. They continue to lower until they come to a stop at the buckle of my belt.

Jesus. I need to slow this train down or I'm going to embarrass myself.

I lean down to kiss her, adjusting the monstrous erection trying to escape my pants. Her hand sneaks down between us and she touches herself.

"No way, babe. That's my job." Scooting myself down the bed until I'm eye level with my prize, I place warm, wet kisses along her hip bone and inner thigh, teasing, licking, and biting her until she's shifting restlessly again, her fingers knotting in the blankets at her sides.

"Teddy," she moans.

I bring my mouth where she wants me and groan when I remember how good she tastes. *Yum.* She's perfect.

With one foot flat against the bed and the other rubbing up and down the center of my back, she rocks herself closer, eager for every bit of pleasure I can deliver. And deliver, I do. I'm shameless in my pursuit of her orgasm.

Placing one hand against her stomach, I hold her in place, and with the other, I explore her breasts, caressing and pinching until her breathy gasps grow more needy. I glance up, desperate to see her expression. Those gorgeous full lips are parted and her eyes are focused on the action. *Oh yeah.*

My hips move shamelessly against the mattress, and I don't even care that I'm fucking my bed in heavy, uncoordinated thrusts. I have to move, have to do something before I explode. If Sara is bothered by any of this—my embarrassingly hard dick, or the desperate noises I'm making—she doesn't let on.

Sealing my lips around her, I give a good, hard suck, and her hips jolt as she moans out my name again.

"Are you going to come for me?" I murmur, my tongue moving in slow, sure strokes.

Her head bobs, and she makes a needy sound as I suck again, my tongue tracing her sensitive flesh. And then her hands are in my hair and she's coming. Her body tenses and a curse leaves her lips as her hands tighten around the back of my neck.

Fuck yeah. She's so sexy.

While she's still trembling in my arms, I kiss my way up her body, nuzzling into her neck with soft kisses as my hand works fast to open the front of my pants. Shoving them down only far enough to free myself, I get my hand around my swollen cock, jacking it as her hands run up and down my back and shoulders. A few more lazy tugs and then I'm coming, spilling myself all over her stomach in jet after jet of hot liquid.

I shiver, breathing hard against her neck. "*Fuck.*"

She meets my eyes as I reluctantly lift myself off of her with one arm.

"Sorry," I murmur, glancing down at the mess I made on her.

"Don't be."

A lazy, lust-filled smile overtakes my mouth, and Sara's eyes move from mine down to my still-hard cock that's wrapped in my fist.

"Let me grab something to clean you up," I say, hefting myself up off the bed.

After cleaning myself in the bathroom, I'm back with a warm washcloth that I use to wipe away the remnants of my orgasm from her stomach. I'm not sure if things are about to turn awkward between us, but thankfully, they don't. With a satisfied sigh, Sara gets up and begins dressing while I change into jeans and a T-shirt. She was never one to make sex into something awkward and it's just one more thing I find myself admiring about her.

Once we're both decent, she turns to face me, lifting onto her toes to press a quick kiss to my lips. "Is it okay if I take a rain check on the ice cream?"

I grin down at her. "Of course it is. I'll save you some."

"You're the best."

"Can I drive you home?" I ask, picking up my keys.

She nods and slips into her high heels once again, neither of us mentioning what just took place in my study, or in my bedroom.

As we get in the car for the drive back to her place, one thought skates through my brain on a continuous loop.

The date might have been fake, but the orgasms? Those felt *very* real.

CHAPTER NINE

Sangria and Secrets

Sara

It's Monday morning at Carroll and Associates, and although I've been at my desk sipping cold coffee and staring at a crowded in-box for nearly an hour, I've gotten approximately zero things done. I wish I could say I don't know what's gotten into me, but I'd be lying if I said I couldn't precisely pinpoint what my distraction is. He's six foot three, chiseled as hell, mouth like a Dyson vacuum, and keeps infiltrating my thoughts.

No matter how daunting my email in-box is today, I can't wrangle my mind into focusing on work without it wandering back to Friday night. I had no intention of hooking up with Teddy, but the second he pressed PLAY on that video, I knew my body would betray me.

I told myself it was a long time ago and I'd moved on, but watching us move together on video sent electricity coursing through my veins, the same electricity I felt pulsing through my core the night we hit RECORD. And I couldn't help but act on it.

While I'm still pissed that Teddy lied to me about deleting every copy of our little sex tape, he was right about one thing. That video is hot. Apparently, hot enough for me to want to reenact a scene. But as fun as Friday night was, I need to remember that, above all else, Teddy is my client. And a friend. Which means I need to hit PAUSE on the naughty daydreams and make sure that we're the only two sets of eyes that ever see our little cinematic experiment. Aside from the jerk who hacked into it.

Speaking of . . .

In the midst of my cluttered Monday morning in-box, one message stands out. The random letters and numbers that make up the email address it's sent from are an instant indication that this is the message I've been waiting for. A reply to the cease-and-desist letter I sent.

I open the email and am met with exactly the sort of message I was expecting. He's trying to cash in on this. At least, I assume it's a he.

The message is to the point. The idiot wants a million dollars. In exchange for what? A promise that he won't blast this video all over the world wide web? As if I would trust that a person who breaks into people's personal clouds for shits and grins would keep a promise. That's not how any of this works.

I keep my answer short and sweet.

> My client is offering not to prosecute in exchange for your cooperation. If you choose not to cooperate, we are prepared to press charges. The choice is yours.

It's not my most professional email, but then again, sending threats isn't normally a part of my job description. Unfortunately, this threat is really more of a bluff.

The private investigator I hired has been unable to trace the blackmailer's IP address, leaving us pretty much in the dark on who, or even where, he or she is. As far as lawsuits go, we can't exactly prosecute someone if we can't identify them first, and if they turn out to be outside of the country, this whole mess gets ten times more complicated. Whoever this creep is, they've done their homework on how to cover their tracks.

I heave a sigh, then press SEND on the email. Until I get a response or the PI gets a lead on this guy, there's not much I can do on this case, and I have about a dozen others I need to work on today. I frown at my computer monitor, weighing my options on where to start, but before I can make up my mind, a shadow appears in my door frame. It's David, my boss, clutching a coffee mug and giving me a narrow-eyed stare.

"Good morning, Ms. Dawson. How's that's intellectual property case coming?"

It takes a second for me to even remember which case he's referring to. *Shit.* I am so off my game today.

"I haven't looked at it yet today," I admit with a small smile. "I've been pretty tied up with a few other clients this morning."

A knot forms in my stomach. I shouldn't be lying to my boss, but what am I supposed to say? That I've been too busy reliving my Friday night orgasm to do my job? Although maybe he would understand, because that was one hell of an orgasm.

David gives me a firm nod. "Understood. I hope you can make some progress on that today. We'll be discussing it next week at your review."

My eyes dart to my calendar. *Shit.*

This review, the thing I've been counting down the days to for months, the day I'll bring everything I've got to the table in hopes of walking out of that meeting as a partner of Carroll and Associates, has somehow sneaked up on me. I was hoping that I'd have the promotion in the bag by now, but this morning, I'm not feeling so sure.

Hello, intellectual property case. It looks like you and I are going to be spending the rest of the day together.

"Absolutely. Looking forward to it." I grin as he gives me one more nod and then exits my office.

After logging a full ten hours of uninterrupted work, I sign off for the day and head for the wine bar down the street. I was supposed to meet the girls for happy hour about thirty minutes ago, but better late than never, right?

As I walk up to the bar, I spy Aubree, Elise,

Becca, and Bailey through the window and give them a tiny wave as I tug open the door. They've already divvied up a pitcher of sangria, and I just barely catch the tail end of a story Aubree is telling about a huge anonymous donation that came in today for the charity she works for. As I slide into the booth next to her, I make a mental note to ask her to retell the beginning of the story later.

"Sorry I'm late." I reach for the pitcher and an empty glass, giving myself a heavy pour of sangria. "Work was nuts."

"Isn't work always nuts when you're a lawyer?" Bailey asks, fishing a raspberry out of her drink and popping it between her lips. "How is the state of the legal world today, Sara Dawson, Esquire?"

I smile through my first sip of sangria, the fruity flavor washing away the stress of the workday. "Overwhelming as always."

For half a second, I consider telling them about the sex tape, but opt instead to take another swig of sangria. I said from the start that I wanted to get as few people involved in this as possible, and I'm going to stick to that. It might, however, be a good idea to fill them in on Teddy and me. Better they hear it from me than from some sports gossip website in a few days.

"There's actually something I wanted to tell you guys," I say, circling my straw through the ice in my glass.

All four of them lean in attentively, ready to hear whatever gossip I have to offer. It's been a long time since I've had a secret to share with the girls.

"So I went on a date on Friday," I say, pausing briefly before I drop this bomb on them. "A date with Teddy."

I'm instantly met with four sets of wide eyes and four dropped jaws. I could have guessed that was coming.

"Whoa, hold up." Aubree holds her hand up like she's waiting for the teacher to call on her so she can ask a question. "I'm confused. You and TK? A.k.a. the two members of this friend group who argue more than anyone else?"

I shrug, biting nervously on my straw to keep from spilling all the details on this being for PR purposes. That would involve telling them why we have a public relations scandal to cover up in the first place. But I have no problem with letting them think that Teddy and I are a thing in the meantime.

If anything, it will make this fake relationship a little extra believable to the public.

"He needed a plus-one to his ex's engagement party," I say to explain. It's not a total lie. "I agreed to be his arm candy so he didn't have to show up single to see his engaged ex-girlfriend. And it was fun. We had some drinks, some laughs. No big deal."

I don't exactly relish the idea of lying to my girlfriends, but I'm not totally lying, I decide. I'm telling them half the truth. It's kind of what I do as an attorney—find loopholes and work with them.

Elise gasps. "No big deal?"

"This is so freaking weird," Becca says, shaking her head in disbelief. "You and Teddy are, like, the last two people I would've imagined together."

"We all said the same thing about you and Owen when you started dating," I point out. I'm not sure why I'm so defensive about a relationship that's entirely for show, but for some reason, I am.

"I guess that's fair." Becca backs off, topping off both her own glass of sangria and mine. "I'm just saying. You guys are constantly butting heads. It's hard to imagine you two as a couple."

"We're not a couple," I say, correcting her, although her use of the word *couple* sends a tingle up my spine. I like the sound of that more than I should. "We only went out once. That's all."

"But do you think you're going to go out with him again?" Aubree asks, her eyes glistening with anticipation.

To my surprise, the question releases about a hundred butterflies in my stomach.

"Yeah, I think we will." The smile tugging at my lips grows to a full-blown grin.

After Friday, the idea of going on another date with Teddy, even a fake one, is more than a little exciting. Sure, this is all going to come crashing to an end in a matter of time, but until then, what the hell? Why not have a little fun while it lasts?

After all, I know exactly how fun Teddy King can be.

CHAPTER TEN

Fully Invested

Sara

In the time it takes me to set my phone on my kitchen counter and pop my Thai food leftovers into the microwave, I've heard my phone buzz fifteen times. As in 1-5.

It's a Wednesday night, and after spending a soul-sucking twelve hours at the office today, all I want to do is plop down with my pad Thai and fall asleep on the couch watching reruns of legal dramas—which, by the way, are about a thousand times more exciting than my actual life as an attorney. Instead, it looks like I have fifteen—no, make that sixteen—texts to deal with. And I'm hoping with every fiber of my being that this isn't a work-related emergency. I'm not sure I can scrounge up the energy to deal with one more case file today.

Balancing my bowl in one hand, I snatch up my phone to see what's worth sending sixteen texts about. The group chat with the girls is the culprit of this crime of excessive texting, and when I swipe open my messages, I nearly spill noodles and chicken all over my kitchen floor.

Holy shit. Becca and Owen are engaged.

I stare dumbfounded at the selfie Becca sent us. She's holding up her left hand, a solitaire diamond glistening in the light. Behind her, Owen is absolutely beaming with pride, one arm wrapped tight around Becca's waist as if to indicate that he's never letting go.

God, they're ridiculously cute—like one of those Instagram couples that you think can't possibly be real.

I fire off an enthusiastic reply with as many exclamation points as I can manage, trying to ignore the unexpected pang of jealousy hitting me like an arrow straight to the chest.

Of course I'm happy for Becca and Owen. They're perfect for each other. Yet I can't help but feel slightly envious of what they have. A real, genuine love worth holding on to, till death do you part. Meanwhile, all I've got is a completely fake relationship for the purposes of softening the media blow of a potentially leaked sex tape. Not exactly the textbook definition of romance.

I manage to quiet the green-eyed monster in me long enough to join in the celebration happening in the group chat, oohing and ahhing with the rest of the girls over the enormous rock on Becca's finger. Everyone agrees that we'll have to get brunch on Saturday to celebrate and see just how sparkly the ring is in person, as well as talk wedding plans.

When Aubree volunteers to make the reservation, I duck out of the group message momentarily and open my contacts. I need to text Teddy. Partly because I want to know if he was in on this proposal plan, and partly because I need to feel a little less tragically single right now, even if the best I can do is texting my fake boyfriend.

Seconds after I press SEND to forward him the picture of the happy couple, my phone buzzes with his reply.

`Hell yeah, she said yes!`

I chuckle at his response and quickly type out a message.

Did you know anything about this??

A second later, I get my answer.

Uh, maybe . . .

Plopping down on the couch, I lift a forkful of noodles to my mouth. It makes sense that Owen ran it by the guys before popping the question. If no one else, he would have at least told Justin, probably Becca's parents too. Maybe he told all his teammates; who the heck knows.

My phone lights up with another text.

Are you mad I didn't tell you?

I roll my eyes, a smirk tugging at my lips while I respond.

Of course not. I'm just impressed you didn't spill the beans last Friday after you had a few drinks.

Yeah, right. I can be trusted with a secret, as you well know. Are you still coming to the game Saturday?

A jolt of nerves passes through my body as I look down at his text. Teddy and I settled on Saturday's afternoon game as the perfect opportunity to make our relationship public, since with hundreds of cameras around, it's bound to go viral. I'll be sitting with the other players' girlfriends and wives, rocking TK's jersey, and the rumblings of Teddy King being spotted with a new girl on his arm will be officially confirmed. The thought of being shown on national television overwhelms me, but I know there's no better way to make sure America knows that this Ice Hawks' forward is spoken for.

I type out a reply.

Wouldn't miss it for the world. But for now, I need to eat dinner before I fall asleep. We'll talk details of Saturday tomorrow?

He replies a moment later. Gotcha. Good night, babe.

I hold one finger over those four little letters on my phone screen, *b-a-b-e*, and the tragically single feeling turns to a warm hum in my chest as I drift into a dream where I'm the one flaunting a diamond on my left hand and beaming with happiness.

• • •

Question: What is the correct number of mimosas needed to celebrate one of your best friends getting engaged?

Answer: The limit does not exist.

Saturday mornings are always an absolute zoo at any brunch spot in the city, but we're not eating at just *any* brunch spot today. We're eating at the hottest restaurant for brunch within Seattle city limits. Beneath the airy lighting and plants hanging from the ceiling, all five of us are cozied up at a table meant for four, having taken full benefit of the build-your-own-mimosa bar and what very well may be the world's most impressive selection of pastries. How Aubree managed to snag us a reservation here with only a few days' notice, we may never know.

"Cheers to the woman who finally locked down my brother!" Elise calls out, lifting her glass of water in the air.

We agreed to carpool to the game later, and Elise volunteered to be the designated driver, so she's a no-go on the mimosa bar this morning. I told her I'd stay sober with her in solidarity, so my champagne flute is really more of an orange juice flute. She doesn't have to know the real reason I'm not drinking—I'm too nervous about Teddy and me going public today to stomach anything more than a few sips of OJ.

"Congratulations, future Mrs. Parrish!" Bailey giggles as we all clink our glasses together. "I can't wait for the wedding of the century."

"You guys are going to go down in history as the best bridesmaids ever." Becca smiles, laying a hand on her heart. It's her left hand, of course, and the overhead lights bounce off her ring, casting little rainbows across the table.

"Speaking of which," Aubree says, "I feel like it's our duty as bridesmaids to plan a kick-ass engagement party for you guys."

"But how are you going to outdo this reservation, Aubree?" I tease, sending the group into a giggle fit.

Aubree does an exaggerated toss of her hair, then pretends to dust off her shoulder as she shoots us a devilish grin. "Oh, you know I'll always find a way."

As Bailey pops the last bite of her chocolate-filled croissant between her lips, she holds one finger up in the air to indicate she has something to say. "Sara," she manages to say after she swallows. "Didn't you and TK just go to a fancy-schmancy engagement party? Maybe you could give us some pointers."

My stomach knots. I don't want to make this brunch about my relationship with Teddy. One, I don't want to dive into those details in front of everyone, and two, this morning is all about Becca, not me.

"We can talk about it later," I say, trying to limit the dismissive tone in my voice. "Personally, I want to hear more about when Becca thinks they're going to set a date."

Becca takes the bait on my conversation topic switch, her face lighting up with excitement as she dives headfirst into a full-on defense of winter weddings, describing just how magical they can be.

The tension releases from my shoulders. Crisis averted. The less I have to talk about my relationship with Teddy, the less nervous I feel about the game. Which, as I glance at my phone, starts in forty-five minutes.

I give Elise a look, urging her to check the time, and she gets the message. We have to get out of here if we're going to make it in time to watch the puck drop.

We split the tab and say our good-byes to Bailey, who is going home to study, and Aubree, who has to make an appearance at a charity 5K for work today. I almost make a comment about how I'll be the only single girl in the group at the game, but I bite down hard on my lower lip and catch myself just in time.

No more Single Sara mind-set. I've got to focus and remember whose jersey I'm wearing and whose arm I'm officially on.

It's a quick drive to the arena, and when we arrive, I make sure to follow a few steps behind Becca and Elise, letting them lead the way through the chaos of vendors and fans. I haven't been to many Ice Hawks games lately, whereas the two of them are here more nights than not. They know their way around much better than I do.

Our second-row seats are so close to the ice, it feels ridiculously indulgent, and I get a little more excited. There are a few familiar women in the seats next to ours, each of them sporting an Ice Hawks hat, jersey, or both. I recognize one of them as Coach Dodd's wife, and the other two greet Becca and Elise with hugs before making their way to me.

"I'm Sara, Teddy King's girlfriend. Number four," I say, shaking each of their hands. It's the first time I've said it out loud. *Teddy King's girlfriend.* I hope it sounded believable.

"Girlfriend?" Elise says on a gasp. "So, you two are official already?"

"She's wearing his jersey, Elise." Becca gestures to the giant number on my back. "It doesn't get much more official than that. Now, are we getting soft pretzels or not?"

While Elise chaperones a tipsy Becca on her way to the concession stand, I grab a seat next to the coach's wife, making polite hockey-related small talk.

"Have you come to see him play before?" she asks. "He's a wicked forward."

I'm instantly reminded of all the college hockey games I used to drag my roommate to. Even when she was busy studying, I would go by myself, not wanting to miss a chance to see Teddy play.

"It's been a while," I admit with a smile. "I'm excited to be here."

And it's true. To be sitting here with the exclusive club of women dating the players? It's exciting. Or maybe nerve-racking. But I'm not going to take the time to sort that out. We're just a few minutes from puck drop, and before long, Elise and Becca are back, pretzels in hand and ready to cheer on their guys.

"It's so good to have you here," Elise tells me between bites of pretzel. "Trust me. You're going to love watching the game with the girls."

My pulse quickens as I force a smile. Because the truth is, I really do think I'm going to love it. Probably a little too much. But I can't get used to this.

What happens after this whole crazy sex-tape situation blows over? Do Teddy and I tell all our friends the truth? Or do we pretend to break up? Whatever we decide, I certainly won't have a spot with the hockey girlfriends anymore.

I hope that after all is said and done, maybe things will go back to normal. If I can just stop noticing how handsome Teddy is, maybe we can go back to being friends again. We pulled it off after college. Why should it be any different this time around?

My worrying is interrupted by the announcer's voice booming over the loudspeaker and the whole crowd screaming and jumping to their feet. Player by player, the team skates onto the ice, and when Teddy enters the rink, I lose my mind cheering and clapping as loud as humanly possible.

We're close enough that when I spot the gleam lighting up his eyes as they lock with mine, the chilly arena suddenly feels warmer, like a cozy wool blanket has been placed around my shoulders. As he skates to the other end of the rink, he blows me a kiss, which nearly knocks me over.

Nice play, King. Let's hope the cameras caught that one.

"Oh my God!" Becca squeals, clapping her hands together giddily. "That was so cute. I take back everything I said about not picturing you guys together. You're freaking adorable."

I shrug as if it's no big deal, but on the inside, my heart is working double-time. Because even if that kiss was just for the cameras, it hit me in the feels harder than Teddy's best slap shot.

My reaction to him is unexpected. Unwarranted. Unwanted. We've spent years hanging out in the same circle of friends, so why now am I suddenly so hot and needy for him? Maybe because I know how good he looks naked, how amazing he is with his tongue.

Stop it, Sara. Pull your head out of your ass and quit fantasizing about the hot hockey jock.

Nothing good can come of nurturing my growing little obsession with him. But the more I try to pretend I'm not affected by him, the worse my longing gets. And if I can't get these feelings under control, we're both going to be taking the penalty for it.

As the action starts, my gaze is focused on the ice, chasing the players and the puck with every fierce move they make. I've been to Teddy's games many times over the years, but being here tonight is a different experience, maybe because I'm closely watching everything and seeing it through a new lens.

Like how bulking ginormous Owen looks with all that gear on. The way their team captain, Grant, stations himself at the end of the bench to tap gloves with the guys coming in off their shift. The way Teddy moves effortlessly, yet so aggressively across the ice. It's a game that requires a lot of stamina and courage, and Teddy is damn good at it.

To say I'm proud would be a massive understatement. But it's the rest of my emotions that have me more than a little on edge.

Taking a much-needed breath, I lean forward in my seat, way more into this game than I ever expected.

CHAPTER ELEVEN

Sexy Little Temptress

Teddy

I can't seem to shake the memory of the last time I was alone with Sara . . . *it wasn't my finest performance.*

I jerked off on her like some hormonal teenager. I'd barely shoved my pants down when I was all but fisting my cock and jerking it against her stomach, coming in under a minute with the taste of her still on my tongue. I doubt that's what LaShonda had in mind when she suggested we begin dating to keep up appearances. *My bad.*

But if Sara is holding this against me, you wouldn't know it. Her fingers curl around my bicep, and she lets out a low laugh at something Asher just said.

Does she know she's turning me on?

Not to mention, she's wearing that lipstick again—that fucking bright pink lipstick that makes the front of my pants too tight.

She came to my game last Saturday, but we didn't go out afterward. The media had caught wind of our *relationship* . . . so, mission accomplished. Sara texted me *good game* when she got home, and I received a pleased email from LaShonda the next morning saying we were all over the media.

While I spent this week traveling for two games in the Midwest, Sara spent the week buried in work. Which means that this is the first chance we've gotten to be together again. I sort of wish we were somewhere quiet, alone, instead of here in this swanky hotel's ballroom. But celebrating Owen and Becca's engagement has won out.

The low lighting and circling waiters carrying trays of champagne and little hors d'oeuvres create a romantic, intimate ambience. In the center of the room are the guests of honor—Owen, tuxedo-clad and beaming with a huge grin, his arm around his new fiancée, Becca, who looks equally as over-joyed, dressed in a long cream-colored silk gown. They look so happy.

Something twists inside me, and I shake away the feeling, leaning down to ask Sara if she'd like another cocktail.

Nodding happily, she presses a kiss to my cheek. "Yes, and one of those little crab puff thingys, please."

I have no idea if that kiss was really for me, or for the benefit of our friends who think we're actually dating.

Taking advantage of the situation, I give her hip a squeeze and leave her with Asher. I don't miss the way his gaze wanders to where my hand lightly gripped her. I guess it's probably a little strange for our friends to see us behaving like a couple, when the entire time they've known us, we've been nothing but platonic.

Smiling like I've got a secret, I wander to the open bar to get us a refill on our gin and tonics.

Our first cocktail disappeared pretty dang quickly after Sara announced that she's made partner at the law firm, a goal she's been working toward for years. Between the celebratory toasts and congratulations, that first round went fast. But Sara, in her typical humble fashion, didn't want to take the spotlight from Becca and Owen's night, and banned us all from mentioning it again—at least for the night. I'm so damn proud of her, though I could burst.

After stuffing a couple of bills into the tip jar, I collect our drinks and wander back toward Sara. This time she and Asher have been joined by Bailey and Elise. Bailey's talking about bridesmaid dresses while Sara nods along dutifully, like a good friend. It's kind of amusing.

"Have I told you how gorgeous you look tonight?" I murmur low near her ear. "Prettiest girl in the room."

I'm rewarded with an elbow to my ribs and can't help but chuckle. She's feisty, and I love it.

I'm trying to distract myself and keep the mood light, because the alternative is focusing on the fact that if our sex tape leaks, her promotion will be pulled back faster than a goal shot during a timeout. It's not something I want to think about.

"You look handsome too," she finally whispers, giving me a sly smile.

I place my hand at her lower back and lean close again, appreciating the delicious scent of her bodywash. "I guess engagement parties are becoming our thing."

She nods, meeting my eyes with a sultry expression. "Two in what . . . four weeks?"

I nod. "We're on a roll."

She shoots me a wicked look. "Just don't drink the water."

Gazing at her curiously, I start to wonder about that comment. "Why? Are you scared we'll be next?"

Her lips part, and she watches me but doesn't reply. Something about her reaction shakes me and causes my stomach to sink to the floor, like the idea of ending up with a guy like me would be the worst thing she could imagine.

"Hey, if anyone's next, it's me and Justin," Elise says, placing one hand on her hip and giving us a pointed look. "We've been together longer than Becca and Owen. And you guys have only been dating for like four minutes."

Sara laughs and turns toward Elise, where they get into a serious discussion about how long each couple has been dating, and a host of other things that I would classify squarely under the category of girl talk. I do my best to tune it out.

Becca and Owen escape from the pack of relatives that have been holding them hostage and make their way over toward our group.

"Damn, look at that rock!" Bailey says dramatically, shielding her eyes when Becca gets close.

Owen looks so proud he could burst, and Becca lets out a low laugh, holding out her left hand for everyone to inspect her engagement ring.

While they talk about setting a date, I fixate on something else.

"Don't drink the water."

That comment is still bouncing around in my brain as we're encouraged to take our seats for dinner. I pull out Sara's chair and she lowers herself into it, sitting between me and Bailey. Also at our table are Asher, Justin, and Elise, the rookie Landon, and our team captain, Grant. I notice he's drinking water rather than a cocktail like everyone else. He's certainly more disciplined than I am. Owen and Becca are sitting at a nearby table with their parents—something about getting the families to meet for the first time.

The evening passes too quickly, and after feasting on steak and crab cakes, Sara is seated beside me in my car and we're cruising toward her place. She doesn't seem to realize that her comment at the party struck a chord within me. After fiddling with the radio until she finds a song she likes, Sara hums along to the music, looking out the window at the passing streetlights.

When we reach her place, I park at the curb and turn in my seat to face her.

"Are you coming in, or what?" she asks, her voice low and seductive.

My mouth twitches. "Are you going to try and take advantage of me, Dawson?"

"I don't think I'm going to have to try too hard, King." She climbs out of the car and walks toward the stairs, and I quickly follow her like a goalie chasing a puck.

We're barely inside the door before my lips are on her neck. The lock clicks behind us, and I press her back against the wall, lifting her chin toward mine.

"Been thinking about kissing you all night," I whisper.

"Were you waiting for a formal invitation?"

"Not really." I kiss her hard and deep, desperate for my mouth to be on hers. Sara parts her lips, and the moment her tongue touches mine, my cock jumps to attention.

Her hands wander under my jacket, and she runs her palms down my chest, her breath coming out in sexy little pants. “Bedroom.”

“Yeah,” I say on a groan.

She slips off her heels and leads the way to her room, not bothering to turn on any lights until we reach our destination. Pausing only long enough to flip on a small lamp on her dresser, Sara’s back in my arms, kissing me again within seconds.

My hands skim over her curves, and I make a frustrated sound. “Where the fuck’s the zipper on this thing?”

She chuckles. “On the side.”

Her fingers help mine, and together we draw the dress down over her body until it puddles at her feet and she can kick it off. Dressed only in a pair of nude-colored panties and matching strapless bra, Sara gives me a challenging look.

“About time you lost the suit,” she says.

I happily comply, stripping down so fast that she’s chuckling as she watches me toss everything over the side of the bed, including my black socks. There’s nothing attractive about a naked man still wearing socks.

She crawls toward the end of the bed where I'm seated, and when she drops to the floor between my feet, all the air leaves my lungs at once.

With her blue eyes on mine, Sara lowers her mouth to my cock and presses a soft kiss to the almost painfully swollen tip.

Jesus.

I'm going to disgrace myself.

Realizing most of her lip color has worn off, I touch her cheek, stopping her. "Go get your lipstick."

She looks up at me in confusion.

"Please," I say, and this time she does, hopping up to retrieve the gold tube from her clutch on the dresser. "Put it on."

Sara parts her lips and reapplies the color. Then she stands before me in her panties and bra, her dark hair loose around her shoulders, and those full lips painted a vibrant pink.

Damn. She's stunning.

"Now come here." I crook my finger at her and Sara obeys, crossing the room until she stops before me. My heart rate triples as I watch her sink to her knees again.

Gripping my length with her right hand, she treats me to another soft kiss, then two.

"Get me all messy," I say on a pant.

Watching her kiss a teasing path down the length of me, I forget how to breathe, how to think, how to do anything other than make choking, gasping, pleading sounds for her to take more of me. *Babe, please.* And then she does. Parting those gorgeous lips, she sinks down, and my length disappears into that hot, wet mouth of hers.

Fuuuck.

"That's it," I murmur, touching the soft tresses of her hair while my entire body goes rigid. "Just like that."

Sara dives in with enthusiasm, treating me to the best blow job of my entire life while I watch with a half-lidded gaze.

Lipstick stains on my skin, kiss marks along on my thigh and, *oh fuck*, on my cock. I don't think I'll ever be able to get this visual out of my head. Not that I'd ever want to.

I'm gone for her—big freaking time.

CHAPTER TWELVE

Minty Fresh

Sara

"Feel good?" I ask, batting my eyelashes up at Teddy.

He watches me with half-lidded eyes, his expression smoldering like he's trying to hold himself together. But it doesn't stop the groan that pours out of him as I gently cup his balls with one hand and thumb his swollen tip with the other. I love seeing him like this—so totally blissed out—and knowing it's all because of me.

"Fuck, babe." He shakes his head in disbelief. "Too good."

I lower my mouth again and almost smile—well, if my mouth weren't otherwise occupied, that is. Because Teddy King tastes exactly how I remembered.

As I bob my head in time with his gentle thrusts, the lingering minty taste of his bodywash is all too familiar. He's used the same brand for years now. And with every passing second, with every inch deeper I take him into my mouth, I develop more and more of a taste for peppermint.

I look up at him and suction my lips a little tighter against him. He moans and clutches my hair in response.

God, he's so impossibly sexy when he moans. It makes it nearly impossible to concentrate on what I'm doing. Momentarily, I ease him out of my mouth, working him over with my hand.

His muscles tense, a sure giveaway that he's getting close, and suddenly, all I want in the world is to see him come totally undone for me. My lips part and I welcome him back into my mouth, a return that earns me a low, throaty hum of approval.

"That's perfect." He pants out the words, his eyes slowly sinking closed. "Like that. Nice and slow."

I follow his sexy instructions, taking my sweet time to run my tongue along every inch of his shaft until I'm sucking flirtatiously on the tip. I'm not usually this enthusiastic about having a dick in my mouth, but watching Teddy, who's normally so cool and composed, tense and groan at the mercy of my mouth is more than hot. It's sort of a power trip.

Tonight was a torturous game of *look but don't touch*, and I'd been eager to get Teddy alone, as crazy as it was. And while tonight might have been about Becca and Owen, Teddy was the standout in the crowd. When he got closer, wrapping his big, firm hand around my waist, towering over me with his massive frame, something inside me shifted. A hot pulsing low in my core. And God, he smelled divine. Like soap and cologne and man. Greedily, I drank him in. His broad chest and shoulders, those sculpted biceps pulling at the sleeves of his shirt. I wanted to climb him like a tree. It didn't matter that I told myself he was off-limits; our chemistry was undeniable.

He hardly makes it a few slow moments before I can feel everything in him tighten against me. He can't take it anymore. Fisting my hair in his hand, he plunges into my mouth for a few final thrusts before groaning he's going to come, and then empties himself in wet, hot bursts down my throat.

After, I sit back on my heels and allow him a moment to collect himself, waiting patiently on my knees as he catches his breath and uses his forearm to wipe the sweat from his brow. When his eyes finally flutter open, it's to give me a sexy look that, if I weren't already sitting down, would knock me right on my butt.

"What?" I tilt my head and smirk up at him.

For a second, I don't think he's going to say anything. He runs his tongue over his bottom lip and shakes his head, then finally breaks the silence with a snicker.

"What do you mean, what?" He laughs, still sounding slightly breathless. "You know exactly what."

I shrug. "Maybe. Or maybe I just want to hear you say it."

Teddy cradles my face in his hands, running one thumb along my lower lip. The goose bumps are instantaneous.

"You are absolutely incredible, Sara Dawson. That's what."

Leaning down to my level, he sweeps his lips across mine in a quick, airy kiss, then tugs me up onto the bed next to him.

"Come on. You're the one who made partner,

not me. You should be the one getting treated like royalty."

"Royalty, huh?" I tease, tracing his jawline lazily with my fingertips. His stubble is pleasantly rough against my skin. "Is that how I just treated you?"

"There's not a king in history who has ever gotten head that good," Teddy says, his voice entirely serious. "Guarantee it. If there was, we would've read about it in every freaking textbook."

A bubbly laugh spills from my lips. "Somehow I feel like they wouldn't include oral sex as a critical historic event for students to memorize."

Teddy shrugs. "They would have if it was ever as good as that."

I've got a full arsenal of comebacks that could further this debate, but I don't get so much as half a second to use one.

In one swift movement, Teddy is suddenly on his feet, tugging me to the edge of the bed and taking the same spot on his knees that I occupied moments ago. He tugs my panties down my legs and helps me untangle them from my ankles like he has all the time in the world to worship me. My strapless bra comes next, and then I'm bare before him.

Every ounce of air escapes my lungs as he slides two fingers against me, groaning in appreciation of how wet I am.

"God," he says on a strained sigh. "So wet for me."

And he's right. It's all for him. My eyes sink closed, and I murmur my approval at the soft, exquisite way he's touching me.

"Don't you dare close your eyes," he whispers.

My breath catches as my gaze meets his. His piercing green eyes are hungry, and I'm the only thing on the menu.

He curls his fingers within me, and I buck in pleasure as he applies the perfect amount of pressure to the softest spot within me. He hasn't forgotten my body and or how to give me exactly what I crave. As his fingers move, he lowers his mouth to my center, touching his tongue against me.

Shit. My back arches against my will, and I squirm and shake beneath him, my heart rate climbing until it's all I can do to grab his shoulders and hold on for dear life.

But it doesn't matter how hard I hang on or how desperately I want to make this last, to freeze time in this moment with Teddy working magic between my thighs and me, gripping his muscles tight.

I want to hit PAUSE. To stay here forever. But a few expert laps of his tongue and I'm gone, riding out the hot waves of my orgasm as I come completely undone for him.

My muscles are still twitching with pleasure as Teddy rejoins me on the bed, pulling my body close until I'm folded into him in what has to be the best post-sex cuddle session I've ever had.

Well, the best and the shortest. Just when we find the perfect fit of my curves against his frame, his stomach grumbles to life against the small of my back. I shift out of his hold to turn over and shoot him a smile.

"Hungry?"

He smirks. "Always. But I may have worked up a bit of an appetite. Any chance I can raid your pantry?"

I chuckle. I love his honesty. Love how casual and relaxed we are together. "Go for it."

While Teddy tugs his dress pants back on, I forgo the dress I had on earlier for a much comfier option. Cue the slouchy, worn-in T-shirt and run ning shorts.

For a second, I consider suggesting that he could keep extra clothes at my place for these kind of situations—I have an empty drawer in my dresser practically calling his name—but I catch myself before the words come out of my mouth. Leaving clothes at each other's apartments is a telltale sign of a serious relationship. For a fake relationship for the public eye? Not so much. But with all the faking it for our friends along with the cameras, I'm starting to lose track of what's real and what's not.

In the kitchen, I head for the fridge and grab myself a bottle of water, gesturing for Teddy to make himself at home in the pantry. And he does. Once I show him where to find the snacks, he wastes no time rummaging through my shelves.

"Do you have anything that's not organic?" he half whines, pushing aside the bags upon bags of dried fruit and nuts I keep my kitchen stocked with.

I set my water on the counter and fold my arms over my chest, instantly on the defensive. "What's wrong with organic? I think there are some tortilla chips and salsa in there somewhere."

Teddy chuckles as he snags the unopened bag

of chips from the back of the cabinet. "You're telling me you're a lawyer, one of the most stressful jobs out there, and you don't even have comfort food to come home to?" He shakes his head in disbelief as he pops the seal on the salsa jar. "I'm going to have some comfort food delivered here to keep us both sane."

Between the two of us, we manage to demolish most of the bag of tortilla chips and half the jar of salsa in under thirty minutes. I had almost forgotten what it takes to feed an athlete. By the time we're down to the crumbs and broken chips, it's nearly midnight, and I can't hold in my yawns anymore.

"I guess I should hit the road." There's a twinge of disappointment in Teddy's voice as he checks his watch and springs to his feet.

I nod, trying to conceal the fact that I'm a little bummed to see him go. I had fun with him tonight. We both try to make our kiss good-bye last as long as possible before Teddy eventually has to go, promising he'll text me tomorrow.

After his car pulls down my street and out of view, I head for the bathroom to wash my face and brush my teeth. I'm silently congratulating myself for maintaining my nighttime routine despite my exhaustion. I could have fallen asleep halfway through dipping a chip in salsa.

But I make it to bed, pleased to discover that my sheets still smell a little bit like Teddy. A comforting minty smell that lulls me straight to sleep.

CHAPTER THIRTEEN

Reality Check

Teddy

"You looked good out there today," Coach Dodd says in passing, his eyes barely lifting from his phone, even if the tone of his voice is as sincere as I've ever heard it.

Tired after the grueling practice, I grin and thank him, then turn for the weight room to squeeze in some resistance training with a little more pep in my step than before.

"Slay all day," Asher says, tipping his chin at me when I enter. He's about as subtle as an elephant in a phone booth, but I guess he heard Dodd's praise.

"I guess I'm just well-fed today or something." I shrug.

Asher chuckles and grabs two fifty-pound

dumbbells, stationing himself at a bench across the room. “Whatever you need to tell yourself.”

He’s right, though. I performed well today, finding Parrish’s five-hole twice in practice, which almost never happens, and then assisting the rookie Landon with a nice goal too. Hell, I even kept up with some of the younger guys when we did suicide sprints, which I normally hate.

The truth is, you’ve got to be *on* in practice when you know there are two teams looking at you—one of which being Denver, the city where my aging grandfather lives. I can’t afford to be sloppy or get complacent, even if I am having a hard time picturing myself moving across the country just when things have gotten interesting between Sara and me.

Obviously, the chemistry between us is combustible, but it’s more than that. We have a lot in common too—high-pressure jobs, the same group of friends, aging parents, and a dirty sense of humor. Not to mention our odd love of chain restaurants . . . which reminds me, I should totally surprise her at some point and drop off chicken wings at her place. I can only imagine the smile that would greet me if I did.

My cell phone vibrates from the floor beside

me, and I grab it, answering it immediately when I recognize the Colorado number. "Hello?"

"Mr. King? I'm calling about your grandfather Joe," a female voice says firmly.

My stomach drops and I sink onto the nearest bench. "Is he okay?"

Asher shoots me a worried look from across the gym, and I squeeze my eyes closed, mentally preparing myself for horrible news.

"He's okay. But he took a little tumble this afternoon. An ambulance transported him to the hospital to make sure he didn't dislocate his hip in the fall. He's okay now. Nothing is broken; he's just a little shaken up."

My hand shakes as I clutch the phone to my ear. "Can I speak to him?"

"He's napping now, but if you call back in a couple of hours, then absolutely. I know he'd love that."

"Okay. I'll call back. This number?" I ask, double-checking.

"Yes, that's right."

"Thanks for the call. And I'll, uh, try to fly out

there in a few days." I have no earthly idea how I'll make that happen with back-to-back away games coming up, but I'll try to make it work.

At this, the nurse pauses, going quiet for a moment. "With all due respect, Mr. King, I'm familiar with your position and your travel schedule. I may be overstepping now, but I really don't think your grandpa would expect you to do that."

At this, I can't help but smile. "Yeah, he'll probably be a pain in the ass about it when I show up, but I'll be there all the same." As soon as I can figure out how the hell I'm supposed to fly to Colorado with my already hectic travel schedule.

"Okay. Sounds like a plan, Mr. King." Her voice is chipper and slightly mollifying.

"Thanks," I say, ending the call, and try not to punch the weight bench as I heft myself up.

"Everything all right?" Asher asks, handing me a bottle of water while his eyebrows dart up on his forehead.

"My grandpa. But it sounds like he'll be all right."

Asher gives me a curious look. I realize I've never told anyone about my grandpa's failing health and I'm not even sure why—like if I don't talk about it, it won't be real. Except that's not true, because I mentioned it to Sara on our first date.

And that's when it hits me with the full force of a cross-check into the Plexiglas.

Even though things with Sara have been exceptionally fun, I have to keep my eye on my goal, which is to hopefully get traded and move to be closer to Gramps. There's no way I can be there for him when I'm over a thousand miles away.

Hell, even the kind nurse told me that in not so many words—don't bother coming in a few days, because this latest episode will be all but forgotten by then, and we'll probably be on to some new health scare.

Welcome to the world's suckiest decision. Stay here in a city I love with a girl I might have a shot with, or do the right thing and go take care of the only family I have left.

It's really not a decision at all.

CHAPTER FOURTEEN

Bridesmaid Dresses and Blog Posts

Sara

"Ballet slipper or petal pink?"

Maybe it's just the fluorescent lighting in this bridal shop, but the two dresses Becca is holding up in front of us look nearly identical in color. Or at least they do to me.

Don't get me wrong, they both are absolutely gorgeous, but I can't spot a single difference between the two, even if I squint. They both have long, flowy skirts and tight bodiccs held up by delicate lace straps, and are both roughly the shade of a brand-new ballet slipper. Stunning. Subtle. And, if you ask me, completely the same. But she swears they are two different colors. If I didn't know better, I'd think Becca was pulling a prank on her bridesmaids.

"Seriously, guys," Becca says, jutting out her lower lip. "I can't decide. Which one do you like better for your bridesmaid dresses?"

The look in her eyes is desperate and expectant as the four of us shift our gazes from one to the other. It feels like Becca is asking us to compare apples to oranges, but from what I can see, we're comparing apples to slightly riper apples.

After a longer than comfortable silence, Elise is the first to pipe up, clearing her throat. "Um, which one is which?"

I breathe a sigh of relief. Thank God I'm not the only one who can't tell.

"Petal pink has to be the one on the left, right?" Bailey asks, but the hesitation in her voice suggests that it's a complete guess.

"Right," Becca says, then scrunches her nose. "Wait, your left, right? Or my left, which is your right?"

Oh Lord. I'm getting a headache just trying to keep up. If we spend another hour of this day comparing identical pink dresses to each other, I'm going to go completely out of my mind.

"Why not flip a coin?" I say gently. "They're

both so beautiful, and we'd be happy to wear either one. But one pink versus another isn't nearly as important as the fact that you and Owen are going to be *married* at the end of this, right?" I smile, trying to be helpful.

I can feel the rest of the girls hold their breath at once, waiting to see the bride's reaction. Luckily, it's a positive one. Her tight-lipped expression softens into a smile.

"You're so right, Sara." Becca laughs. "Thank God one of us can stay levelheaded during all of this, because I sure as heck can't."

I let out a soft sigh.

Bailey digs into her purse and emerges with a quarter between her fingers. "I've got a coin. Do you want to do the honors?"

Becca eyes the quarter, then returns the dresses to the rack and giddily rubs her hands together, offering one palm out to Bailey so she can hand over the coin that will decide our fates as bridesmaids.

"Heads, ballet slipper; tails, petal pink," Becca says, then balances the quarter on her thumbnail and flips it. It bounces off of Aubree's shoe and lands on tails.

"Petal pink it is!" Becca says, sporting a proud grin for having made a decision.

Elise laughs. "Okay, but my question still stands. Which one is that?"

All five of us erupt into giggles as we descend upon a rack of petal-pink dresses, holding up different necklines that we think will look best. As I slide hanger after hanger along the rack, I solemnly promise myself that I will skip all this nonsense on my big day and let my bridesmaids wear whatever the heck they want.

That is, if I ever have a wedding. And that's a big *if*, seeing as my current relationship is nothing more than a publicity stunt. Well, a publicity stunt with some very unexpected side effects.

Our relationship may be pretend, but I haven't had to do too much pretending around Teddy lately. Things with him have felt so natural. The last night we spent together, I don't know if I had more fun in the bedroom or just sitting and talking with him over chips and salsa.

Sexually and emotionally, something about us just clicks. And I think Teddy feels the same way, unless I'm reading him wrong. But I am pretty perceptive. Except, I guess, when it comes to spotting the difference between petal pink and ballet slipper.

My phone buzzes in the back pocket of my jeans, and when I see it's Teddy, I can't stop the smile from spreading across my face. He's been dealing with some messy stuff with his grandfather, which I totally get, but it means we've been talking a little less frequently lately.

"Ooh." Bailey giggles, wagging her eyebrows at me suggestively. "I know that smile. Somebody got a text from her man."

"I'll keep it quick," I promise, stepping back from the dress rack. I don't want to dishonor the sacredness of a girls' day, but they all have been thoroughly filled in on Teddy's grandpa's situation. This could be something important.

Turns out, it is important. But not for the reason I expected.

Check it out. We made the hockey blogs.

My eyes widen as three more texts from him pop up, each one a link to a different blog featuring pictures of us leaving the rink together hand in hand. The best part? I was having a damn good hair day.

I look a little closer and can't help but notice the way Teddy is gazing down at me. His expression is so relaxed and happy. I feel a little breathless.

This plan is totally working.

I fire off an excited response to Teddy. `LaShonda is a PR genius!!! We'll have to celebrate.`

His reply comes a second later. `Date tonight?`

Oh.

It's not what I was expecting, but I can't say *yes* quickly enough.

Becca has to run ten miles tonight to stay on her marathon training program, so we already agreed our girls' day would wrap up before dinner, leaving my evening totally free. Still, I'll have to get out of here relatively quickly if I'm going to look presentable enough to be caught on camera tonight.

But when I ask him where we should go to have our best shot at being spotted by the press, his answer surprises me.

No cameras tonight. Just you and me. Want to cook dinner together? I can pick up ingredients.

A warm tingle dances across every nerve in my body. He wants to see me tonight. Not for the press, the cameras, or the big PR plan. Just me and him, cooking dinner, enjoying each other's company. And to me, that's better than any fancy dinner money could buy.

That sounds perfect. Your place or mine? I reply.

His answer comes a second later. Mine. See you tonight.

CHAPTER FIFTEEN

Playing House

Teddy

I'm not a very smart man.

If I were, I wouldn't be torturing myself like this. Playing house, pretending this way with Sara . . . I know it's not smart, but somehow it's all I want in the world tonight.

She's due here in twenty minutes, and I couldn't be more excited. This is definitely the highlight of my week. After practice, a workout, and then a nap, I shopped for groceries and then showered again to make sure all the parts I want her mouth and hot skin all over are nice and smooth.

Thankfully, my cleaning lady was here today, so I don't have anything to clean up. My place is immaculate. My counters are now littered with the ingredients for tonight's dinner, and I have low music playing on the surround-sound system. I check the display and see the low, moody song playing now is titled "You're Somebody Else." It makes me pause for a moment as my brain spins.

Right now, I wish I could be somebody else. Maybe that twenty-one-year-old guy who was reckless and impulsive—the one who did what he wanted without fear of the consequences. The one who spent a lot of time with Sara laughing and having hot, sweaty sex.

If I didn't have to worry about what came after, I would pursue this relationship with Sara with every ounce of my being. If I didn't have the trade or my grandpa's health hanging over my head, I would go all in. It wouldn't even matter that she isn't looking for a serious relationship—I would woo and push and win her over so hard.

I take a deep breath, starting to regret telling her we'd cook. I'm so distracted by thoughts of later that I'm liable to chop off a finger or start a small kitchen fire. Takeout would have been a lot easier. Instead, I have the ingredients for steak Caesar salad.

When Sara texts me a few minutes later that she's stepping into the elevator, I meet her in the hallway just as she's stepping off. I cleared her with the building's security when she agreed to become my lawyer.

"Are you wearing sweatpants?" is the first graceless thing out of my mouth. *Shit. Smooth, Teddy.*

Sara only laughs. "Duh. Why *wouldn't* I be wearing sweatpants?"

She's dressed in a pair of baggy gray sweatpants with the drawstring tied at her waist, and her off-the-shoulder white T-shirt is half-tucked into the front of those ridiculously comfortable-looking pants.

My eyes finally lift to hers. "That's an excellent point."

I invited her here to enjoy a casual night in. We both dress in suits way too often, and she has every right to be comfortable. And even though I seem to have a hard time remembering it, we're not actually dating. This is a PR stunt to protect the interests of my team and sponsors in case I find myself in the middle of a massive scandal.

"You look nice," she says, leaning close to give me a friendly one-armed hug.

I wrap both my arms around her and lift her

feet from the floor. "So do you," I say, finally releasing her.

"I'm supposed to believe that after you just shamed me for wearing my PJs?"

"Wasn't shaming you, babe. You took me by surprise, is all. You're always so buttoned up."

"True. But it's my night off. I wanted to be comfortable."

I nod as she follows me inside. "As you should. Honestly, you're a genius. Hell, I might change too."

"You should definitely join me in comfort-town." She nods.

It's after this conversation that we end up in my kitchen, me dressed in a pair of black athletic pants and a black T-shirt, instead of jeans and the button-down I had on earlier.

Sara is perched on a stool at the counter, and two steaks sizzle side by side in a cast-iron skillet on the stove. I grab a bottle of champagne I've had chilling all afternoon and pull out the cork with a loud pop.

"What are we celebrating?" She gives me a curious look.

"Your promotion, of course."

"I thought we celebrated that the other night." She winks.

"Maybe I want to celebrate you all over again."

"You're sweet."

Not hardly. "You worked your ass off, babe. You're incredible." I pour two glasses of bubbly and offer her one. "Cheers to kicking ass."

She grins and takes a sip of the champagne. "I guess we're both at the top of our game."

She's right, and it's a stark reminder that we both have so much to lose.

I merely nod and take a long gulp of champagne.

"Is it true that you might be traded?" she asks a little while later.

"You read the sports column now?"

She shrugs. "When I have reason to. Is it true?"

I look away, unable to meet her eyes. "Might be. I really don't know for sure yet."

"Why didn't you say anything?"

I push my hand into my hair, stalling for time. "That's a good question."

Truthfully, I know it has something to do with the fact that I didn't want to give her a reason to doubt us, or scare her off before we even have a chance to get started. She might be doing this because my PR rep asked her to, and sure, that's why I agreed initially too.

But from our very first date, something changed. Hell, if I'm being totally honest, maybe it happened before that.

That day in the locker room when Owen told the guys he was planning to propose sort of threw me for a loop. Most of the older guys on the team are married, some have a couple of kids, but before Justin and Elise started dating last year, none of us in our group even had a girlfriend. And now two of my best friends are in serious relationships, and one is getting married.

I was never the type to go out looking for a relationship, but the more time I've spent with Sara, laughing and kissing—hell, even this, listening to her talk about work while I cook—is pretty damn nice and makes me realize I want more.

"I guess I didn't say anything because I'm not

sure what will happen yet, and I figured it was better not to speculate."

She nods. "You didn't want to jinx it?"

I tilt my chin. "Something like that."

I flip the steaks while she fills me in on the dynamic at the law firm, from the lowly associates to the power-hungry partners. Then I get to work on whisking the five ingredients for the salad dressing.

"Yum. Are you making homemade Caesar?"

I nod. "It's pretty easy. If I hadn't learned to cook living with my grandpa, I probably wouldn't have eaten."

She softens, smiling at me. "Well, I'm impressed. Honestly, Teddy, this is sweet of you. The champagne. The steaks. This is the most perfect night in."

The soft expression in her eyes makes something inside me squeeze. "Looks like you could use a refill," I say, nodding toward her empty glass.

"Sure. I can handle one more glass."

"Did you drive?" I ask, retrieving the wine bottle.

She nods.

"Well, you're more than welcome to stay the night if you want another glass later."

Her expression stays neutral as I refill her glass.

Even though I'm dying to know how she feels about that idea, I stay quiet. A smart man knows not to push his luck, even though the idea of spending the entire night with her in my bed is enough to turn my lower half to stone.

I toss the chopped romaine lettuce, sliced cucumbers, and tomatoes into the same bowl I've just finished whisking the dressing in, and pull the steaks out of the pan to rest. Once everything is ready, we carry our feast over to my seldom-used dining table and dig in.

"This steak is perfect," she says, slicing herself another bite.

"I think the last time I ate at this table was the last time my grandpa was in town."

Sara smiles. "Don't tell me you're one of those typical bachelors who eats standing over the sink."

I chuckle. "Guilty."

She shakes her head, but she's still smiling. "Do you cook for yourself like this every night?"

I read into the words she doesn't say . . . *A girl could get used to this.*

Forking a bite of salad, I shake my head. "Nah. I eat a lot of eggs during the week, maybe a quick omelet after practice, or I call in a takeout order from the market downstairs."

"Edelman's?" she asks, and I nod. "What's your go-to?"

"Promise not to laugh?"

"Sure." She grins.

"Caesar salad.

She laughs anyway. "With chicken?"

"Salmon, actually. I read somewhere it's good for inflammation and muscle recovery."

After dinner, Sara insists on loading the dish-washer since I cooked. I don't put up much of a fight because the sight of her in my kitchen, looking so at home in her sweatpants and her hair loose, renders me momentarily speechless. She looks comfortable and relaxed, the vibe so chill and domestic.

Is this what Owen has with Becca, and Justin has with Elise?

Shit. I'm suddenly more than a little jealous.

It's in this moment I realize that I've never had a woman here like this. I've brought hookups home before, sure, but I'm usually seeing how fast we can both get off so I can get her gone.

As I wipe down the counters tonight, I'm trying to think of ways I can talk Sara into staying.

Once the dishes are done, I grab the champagne bottle and refill her glass. Sara watches me quietly. When she accepts the glass and takes a sip, it's with the silent understanding that she'll be spending the night.

"You have a guest room, right?" she asks, her voice soft.

I lean in closer. "If you stay, you and I both know it'll be in my bed, babe."

I don't miss the way her gaze darkens as she meets my eyes. A silent, tense moment passes between us. I want to kiss her, but I don't—not just yet.

"Actually, I just realized I've never given you a proper tour."

"I'd love one," she says, recovering.

I bought this place last year, but I rarely have people over. Owen and Justin share an apartment in the same building a few floors down, and that's where people usually congregate when we hang out. There, or Asher's place when he hosts the poker tournaments he's fond of.

While Sara sips her champagne, I lead the way, heading toward the terrace off the living room. She already saw the study when our erotic video made its premier at the end of our last date. We end up in my room a few minutes later and then into the adjoining bathroom.

"Holy shit, this master bath is insane," she says, wide-eyed. There are two vanities and a separate water closet, a free-standing tub that I've never used, and a glass-enclosed shower with four showerheads.

"Yeah, it's a little ridiculous."

She holds her arms straight out at her sides and does a little spin. "This is the size of my bedroom."

We end the tour back in my bedroom, where I haven't bothered to turn on a light since the dim hallway light provides enough light to see by.

"And this is where the magic happens," I joke.

She smirks, pushing aside the crumpled white duvet that's been flung haphazardly across the mattress. "I can see you still don't make your bed."

"God, no," I say earnestly. "Total waste of time."

Her mouth lifts in a half smile as she watches me.

"Did you want dessert? I still have that peanut butter ice cream we didn't get to the last time."

My brain lodges on the words *last time* . . . That night we were too busy getting it on in my bed—which looms a mere three feet away. A detail my dick hasn't failed to notice.

"I think I'm in the mood for something else."

I take one step closer, my dick getting harder by the second. "Oh yeah?"

"Yeah," she says, her eyes flashing with heat.

Moving closer, I take the glass from her hand and set it on the table beside my bed. Then my hands are cupping her cheeks so I can draw her forward, bringing her lips to mine.

Our mouths meet, softly at first, our kiss tentative. But then her lips part and she brings one hand to the back of my neck, threading her fingers into my hair, and it's all the encouragement I need.

At the first wet pass of her tongue against mine, I taste champagne, and her, and a choked gasp escapes me. And then my hands are on her hips, dipping underneath the waistband of her sweatpants until I can grip the curves of her ass in my hands.

Using my grip on her, I haul her close until she can feel the hot, hard evidence of my arousal between us.

"Teddy." She gasps when my mouth meets the sensitive skin of her neck.

"Yeah, babe?"

"I want you," she says, sighing. "All of you."

"Then have me." Urging her hand between us, I press it over my erection, and Sara groans and gives me a firm squeeze.

"You have the perfect dick," she murmurs as a bolt of electricity zaps down my spine.

"It's available at any time," I say with a groan.

"Stop talking," she says, stroking me again through my pants.

I'm damn good at following instructions. My

mouth gets to work, kissing and sucking and nibbling at each new inch of skin I expose as Sara is methodically stripped of her T-shirt and bra. She drops back onto the bed, working her pants off as she shimmies up the mattress toward the pillows.

"Are you coming?" she asks, watching me with a hooded gaze.

CHAPTER SIXTEEN

Everything

Sara

Teddy is standing before me, and all the air feels like it's been sucked from the dimly lit bedroom. I'm finding it really freaking hard to breathe.

A lazy, confident smile spreads across his face, and his T-shirt does nothing to hide all that well-defined muscle.

I draw an unsteady breath, watching as he undresses.

I've always known how big and muscular he is. Believe me, it's ingrained in my mind, but watching him strip just for me is messing with my head. Watching those muscles flex and jump as more and more smooth, tanned skin comes into view is torturous, and I never want him to stop torturing me.

And when he gives his pants and boxers a shove, and I see his thick erection ready just for me? It's too much, and not enough all at once. I can't wait to get my mouth and my hands all over his deliciously sinful body, but more than anything, I can't wait to feel him inside me again.

He grins when he catches me watching with lust-filled eyes. "See something you like?"

"Don't be dense. Get over here." I crook my finger at him, beckoning him forward.

Keeping my walls up is the only way to make sure I don't do something stupid like fall in love with him. And cheeky quips and mocking jokes are the best way I know how to do exactly that. Because a man like Teddy would be so damn easy to fall for, and I know there would be no coming back.

It was a lifetime ago that we were together like this. Back when he was the hot, goofy hockey player who made me laugh until my stomach ached and always wore a big smile just for me. It was forever ago, but my body's reaction to him right now makes it feel like it was just yesterday.

What Teddy doesn't know is that the laughs

we shared in college meant the world to me. I was young and terrified of failing. I was the first in my family to go to college and on a full academic scholarship. He'd provided the best kind of stress relief, both in and out of the bedroom, and for that I would forever be grateful. Just being near him was cathartic, and to be honest, it still is.

Teddy edges closer to the bed before crawling up over me and bringing his lips to mine in a tender kiss.

Kissing him now, I realize why his kiss has stayed with me all these years. His mouth is soft, yet firm and insistent, and he kisses with the same skill he plays hockey, which is to say at a pro level.

The warmth of his tongue touching mine takes me right back to all those years ago—tucked into his narrow dorm-room bed, feeling the heavy weight of him pressing into me, and the sensation of his hot breath on my neck when he told me he was about to come.

"Where'd you go?" he asks, eyeing me curiously.

I blink up at him, my cheeks flushing under the intensity of his gaze. "Hmm? Nowhere. Sorry. What were we talking about again?"

Teddy laughs, the sound deep and way sexier than a laugh has any right to be.

Threading my fingers behind his neck, I steer his mouth back to mine, his smile still lingering as our lips meet. He's intoxicating, his peppermint scent swirling and mixing with the champagne on his tongue.

And in an instant, I'm drunk on him. No one has ever affected me quite like this, and while I may not understand it, I can't get enough. I tug him closer, desperate to feel his skin against mine. Even an inch of space between us feels like a mile right now, and I want nothing between us.

As our kiss deepens, Teddy's right hand moves between us, and a breathy moan escapes my lips as he drags one finger lazily through me.

"Jesus, babe, so damn wet," he growls against my neck.

I rock my hips ever so slightly, and he takes my cue to keep touching me. Gently, he eases two fingers into me, and my gasp tears through the bedroom. I move against his hand, desperate for more contact.

"What do you want?" he asks, offering his suggestion by curling his fingers and tilting his hips so the pressure of his erection pushes against my belly.

I inhale sharply, trying to find the words to tell him what he already knows.

No, it's not what I want, it's what I *need.* I've waited enough years to feel him inside me again. But now, with us stripped completely bare in his bed, I think waiting even another minute might do me in.

When I finally steady my breath enough, my response comes out somewhere between a sigh and a confession. "Everything."

He shifts his weight over me, adjusting until his gaze is level with mine. "Everything?"

I float one hand down to his length and brush my palm against him, feeling him grow even harder against my touch. "Yes. I want you, all of you."

He brushes his lips against mine, lingering there, close enough that I can feel his exhale. "Your wish is my command."

He steadies his weight on one muscular arm, the other reaching for his bedside table. It takes me a moment to realize what he's doing, but when I do, I tug him back, shaking my head.

"I was just going to put on a—"

"I know. But I'm on the pill."

"And I'm clean," he says without missing a beat, and I believe every word he says, because I know he'd never put me in a harmful situation. "We could go without, but only if you're okay with that."

I run my thumb along the gentle curve of his jawline, the scratch of his scruff sending a flutter through me. The last and only time I let a man go without a condom was when Teddy and I filmed our sex tape. It seems only fitting that this time, our first time in years, should be exactly the same.

"I'm more than okay with it. I want to feel you. All of you. Everything."

It's an invitation he seems more than happy to accept.

Once he's resituated himself over my body, I slide my heels up, bending my knees to accommodate him. He strokes himself a few times for good measure, the slightest smile tugging at the corner of his mouth as he positions himself against my opening. Then, inch by delicious inch, he sinks into me, his breath hissing out from behind his teeth.

Holy freaking moly. Teddy King feels every bit as good as I remember, multiplied by a thousand.

I grip his hips, pulling him into me, urging him to move faster, but he resists, keeping his strokes slow and deliberate. My back arches as I meet each of his strokes with the slightest thrust of my own, accepting more of his length each time. The word "fuck" tumbles out of my mouth a few times, but beyond that, I'm rendered speechless. There's no way I can focus on the English language right now.

Actually, I can't focus on anything but the feel of him moving inside me, especially with those hot, abandoned sounds he's making. Or maybe it's the way his warm breath ghosts over my neck, or his strong, calloused hands skim over my curves, squeezing my hips and ass. And his eyes—*God, those eyes*—give me a look that's equal parts hungry and mesmerized as he gradually moves faster and deeper.

"Sara . . ." He groans, reaching down to draw circles around my clit with his thumb.

I twitch beneath him, sensitive to his touch, then settle into his pace, his thumb and his thrusts working together in one perfect, glorious rhythm. It's hypnotic. Perfect.

Everything within me tightens and tenses as he takes me closer and closer to the edge. I'm fumbling to find my grip anywhere—his back, his shoulders, the sheets. There's nowhere I can hold to keep from completely unraveling beneath him.

With one final, whimpered moan, heat pours through me, and I come undone in a tidal wave of pleasure. Teddy follows only moments behind, emptying into me before collapsing into my arms and burying his face into my neck.

"Wow." I sigh, completely breathless, and reach for words I don't have. "That was . . ."

"Everything?" Teddy suggests, lifting his head and pressing a gentle kiss against my collarbone.

I smile. "Yes. Exactly."

"You feel exactly like I remember," he whispers, looking deep into my eyes. "Absolutely perfect."

The heat in my cheeks deepens as I stare at him. "So do you."

After a few minutes of cuddling in our post-sex bliss, Teddy squeezes my thigh twice, as if to pull me back into reality.

"Why don't you go make use of that fancy

shower I've got?" He nods toward his bathroom door. "I'll grab us some snacks and meet you back in bed."

My eyes widen. A chance to use that amazing shower? He doesn't have to tell me twice.

I nod excitedly, then scramble out of bed and toward the bathroom for what will be the best shower of my life. As I clean myself up, my body tingles, reminding me exactly where Teddy has been. I can't stop smiling. I sigh in bliss while all four showerheads pour hot water over my body.

When I return to the bedroom, squeaky clean and wrapped in a fluffy white towel, Teddy is waiting in bed in just his boxers. At the end of the bed is a folded worn-in Ice Hawks shirt, which I assume is for me. On the nightstand is Teddy's post-sex midnight snack of choice—two pints of peanut butter ice cream.

"Please tell me you weren't thinking about that ice cream the whole time we were having sex." I laugh, slipping out of the towel and into the T-shirt. It's nearly a dress on me, but it's soft and comfy and smells like the man who's letting me borrow it. *Yum.*

He shakes his head, patting the space in bed

next to him. “I promise that all thoughts of ice cream were replaced with absolute disbelief that I had the single most gorgeous woman on the planet naked in my bed. Now come on. I can’t eat all this by myself.”

I give him a knowing look as I cozy up next to him. “Um, TK? I think we both know you could take down five pints of ice cream alone. But I appreciate you sharing. Because I can easily eat my own pint.”

He grins as he passes me a spoon and one of the containers, then taps his pint of ice cream against mine. “Cheers. To the best sex I’ve had since our film debut.”

His words slide through me, warming my cheeks. I don’t know if he’s being serious, but the compliment settles into my chest and renders me momentarily speechless.

I pop the lid off and scoop up a spoonful, then slide it between my lips. It’s the perfect amount of sweet with just a touch of salty. Kind of like Teddy.

I guess I like my men the way I like my ice cream. In bed, and all to myself.

• • •

I slip into a dream where Teddy and I are hiking through the Rockies in Denver, so far off the grid that it's only snow as far as we can see. We're laughing and kissing our way up a mountain, our gloved hands intertwined. And then suddenly, Teddy's phone starts ringing and ringing, so loud that it's echoing through the mountains.

How could he possibly get cell service out here?

A few more rings, and I'm pulled out of my sweet snowy dream and back to reality, where the white blankets are literal, not figurative, and Teddy's phone is buzzing like crazy from its spot on the dresser.

I roll over to face Teddy. His eyes are hooded, but I can still see the look of confusion behind his heavy eyelids. "Did you set an alarm?" I half ask, half groan.

He shakes his head sleepily, confirming what I already know. Teddy has told me numerous times in the past that he never sets alarms, especially not when he doesn't have practice. With all the early morning scrimmages he has, his body wakes him up naturally at an ungodly hour, regardless of what day it is and whether or not he has anything to be awake for. Which means if he's still asleep, it must be insanely early.

I peek at the clock on the bedside table. Four forty-five a.m. Teddy's a popular guy, but who could possibly be calling him at this hour?

He pushes back the covers and swings his feet over the side of the bed as he rubs the sleep from his eyes. When he grabs his phone and gets a look at the screen, the longest, most frustrated sigh pours out of him.

"Teddy?" I sit up, craning my neck as I try to sneak a peek at his screen. I can't read anything from this distance, but I can tell he has about a million and one notifications.

And suddenly, the pieces start to come together in my head.

There's one very good reason why his phone would be blowing up this early. A very personal reason that we've been doing preemptive damage control on for a few weeks now.

I bite down hard on my lower lip and ask the question I wish I didn't have to ask. "TK? Is it—"

"Yeah." His voice is strained, like he's trying to keep from exploding. "The bastard leaked the tape."

I hug my knees to my chest as I watch Teddy scroll through what looks like hundreds of texts and missed call notifications. The room is spinning, and it feels like my heart is lodged in my throat. No matter how many times I gulp, it won't go back down to my chest where it belongs.

Our sex tape is officially available for anyone to see. Every kiss, thrust, and moan we shared is no longer just ours anymore. It's everyone's. Moments ago, I was lost in a blissful dream, and now? Now I'm living a literal nightmare.

I want to be comforting, to ask if he's all right, but I can't even speak with the tornado of worries spinning through my head right now.

What will our friends think? Worse, what will my parents think?

I shake that one off, reminding myself that Mom and Dad are too old and uninterested in hockey to ever catch wind of this. So that's two people on the planet I don't have to worry about having a completely changed opinion of me. Only seven billion or so left to stress over.

And yet, out of those seven billion people, there's really only one who matters to me in this moment. He's sitting on the edge of the bed, scrubbing one hand anxiously through his bed head while the other grips his phone, his eyes firmly locked on his screen as the texts continue to pour in.

"Shit."

One little word from him is all it takes for me to understand everything he's feeling. Overwhelmed. Panicked. Defeated. Angry. I'm feeling it all too.

"We're going to be okay," I finally manage to say. It might be a lie, for all I know, but it's the best I can do right now. "I promise, we're going to be okay."

"You're going to be okay," he says, correcting me. "Your name isn't mentioned. The video is just called *Teddy King Sex Tape*. It doesn't say a thing about you. There's no way it will even be on your boss's radar."

I wait for the sigh of relief to come, but it doesn't. My heart remains firmly lodged in my throat, and my shoulders pressed up against my ears.

Sure, I might get off easy. But what about Teddy? How can I relax knowing his whole career might be crumbling right in front of me?

We're in this together because I was an eager

participant when we decided to step into the realm of homemade porn. Sure, I might get by with some mildly uncomfortable feelings if my name stays out of this, but that's nothing compared to the possibility of Teddy losing his offer from Denver and his sponsorship deals.

Logically, we knew the possibility of this happening was extremely high. A cease-and-desist letter isn't enough to keep some random person on the internet from wreaking havoc on the life of a hugely successful—and let's not forget *rich*—celebrity he doesn't know. I'm sure all he saw was dollar signs when he looked at Teddy.

I was clearly living in a fairy tale where I thought this creeper would just magically disappear. Poof. No more sex tape, no more threatening emails, no more threat of my sex life being available with a couple of clicks on the internet. Our little PR scandal cover-up plan would all be for nothing, and I would be okay with that. Because I'd still have this. Whatever this is that Teddy and I have going on.

But that's the thing about fairy tales. They're about as real as the dream I just woke up from.

Teddy's phone starts ringing again, and his shoulders absolutely deflate. "Shit. It's Coach."

My whole body clenches. It looks like Teddy's Denver dream, the one where he gets to live and play in the city where his grandfather lives, might be coming to an end too.

CHAPTER SEVENTEEN

Nowhere to Hide

Teddy

I'm so angry. I wish I could punch something, scream, and maybe disappear for a day, or fuck, maybe even a year.

Instead, I'm dressed in a suit (LaShonda's idea) and seated across from the Ice Hawks' head coach, inside his office while he lectures me sternly. I've only ever been in Coach Bryant's office one other time, right after I got drafted to the team. Mostly I deal with Coach Dodd, which is a breeze compared to this.

I hear myself say things like *yes, sir*, and *I agree*, and *I'm sorry, sir* while blood pounds in my ears and I suppress my rage.

My sex tape is making the media rounds and has been viewed on all the porn pages, hockey blogs, and entertainment gossip sites. I don't care that people are seeing me; the fact they've seen Sara is what pisses me off the most. I vowed to protect her, swore that video would stay private, and I failed her in the most spectacular way possible.

"I want you laying low for the next couple of weeks. Don't talk to the press. Stay off social media. No going out to bars, and no drunken mistakes. I want you living clean and focused on nothing but hockey. Is that clear?" Coach Bryant asks, his bushy gray eyebrows pulling together into a tight line.

"Yes, sir. We are on the exact same page."

He nods once. "Good to hear."

I hesitate, gripping the armrests of the chair before standing.

"Is there anything else?" he asks.

I clear my throat. "Just, ah, wondering if I'll be starting with my regular line?"

He doesn't give any indication of which way he's leaning, just watches me with a neutral expression over the rim of his glasses, which are pushed down low on the bridge of his nose. "You feel up to that?"

"Absolutely." I have no idea if the crowd will be supportive or mocking given the news that's just broken, but at least it's a home game. Part of me wonders if fans will still be wearing their King jerseys. Hell, maybe they won't let their kids wear them. I really have no idea if I'm a laughingstock or a pariah, or if I'll still have fans in the stands.

"Great. Then I'll see you tomorrow."

I nod and release a breath I didn't know I'd been holding. "See you tomorrow, Coach."

As I head out into the hall with a lump in my throat, I realize that our meeting went better than I could have ever expected. Sure, my offer from Denver is gone, which is no surprise, but Coach didn't bench me, and so far I still have all my sponsorship deals.

But what is making the heaviness in my chest feel a little lighter is that Sara wasn't identified in the video, and we're hopeful she won't ever be. It's a big maybe, but for now she's safe.

Since the news broke this morning, she's worked her ass off to get the video taken down in less than six hours due to revenge-porn laws or something. I'm still not sure of all the details, but I know Sara has been working nonstop while I've been busy getting my ass handed to me. Of course, I had no choice but to take it all, apologizing profusely every chance I got, and praying to God this isn't the end of my career.

After leaving the office, I call Sara, and she picks up on the first ring.

"Hey," I say somberly as I head toward the exit.

"Hey, yourself."

She sounds more chipper than I feel. Here's hoping her cheerful mood rubs off on me.

"How are you holding up?" I ask.

"Me? I'm fine. So far, everything is under control. How did your meeting with Coach go?"

Brutal. "It went okay," I say on a shaky exhale.

She pauses, weighing my words. "Well, that's good. You're not in too much trouble with the team?"

"Coach says I'll still be starting, so I guess not. You want some company?"

"Sure," she says without missing a beat. "Come over."

After we hang up, I head toward her place, stopping briefly to pick up coffee and bagels. I don't dare go into the café; I don't want to show my face. Instead, I cruise through the drive-through window like a coward.

When I arrive with two large coffees and a paper bag, Sara lets me in with a smile. It's not a smile I deserve. I just complicated the fuck out of her life, but a little voice inside me whispers, *She knew what she was getting into when she agreed to this.*

Over coffee and bagels, I listen while she recounts her morning, telling me about the phone calls she fielded and demands she made to get the video removed. I feel weird and sort of detached listening to her describe her actions as my attorney—not as my lover or costar in the video.

"I feel bad you had to work all morning," I say, spotting her laptop on the couch with a pile of legal pads next to it. I think somewhere deep down I knew I would only complicate her life when I came skating back into it. I can't bring myself to regret it, though. The past several hours aside, these past few weeks with her have been incredible.

"It's fine. Don't feel bad. But please tell me the truth about your meeting," she says, pausing with her coffee halfway to her lips as she watches me.

"Was it awful?"

I toss the rest of an uneaten bagel into the bag. My appetite has been nonexistent today. "Denver rescinded their interest," I say sourly. I'm so disappointed in myself because I fucked up my chance to be close to my grandpa.

Sara leans over and rests her hand on my thigh. "Oh, Teddy. I'm so sorry."

I shrug. "I haven't called him yet. Part of me doesn't even want to."

"Why don't you just move him here? To Seattle."

My gaze lifts to hers, and I see a mix of sympathy and confusion staring back at me. "Yeah, I want to. I just need to convince him first. When I brought it up last year, he shut down the idea pretty fast."

"I'm here to help, however I can. We're in this together."

I don't deserve that, but I believe everything she says, and hold on to her words like they're my lifeline.

Although I end up staying the night, we don't have sex. Instead, we watch a movie together, eat a bunch of takeout, and just chill. Once I fall asleep in her bed, I feel at peace for the first time since this mess started.

And it's all because of her.

• • •

Twelve minutes into the most frustrating hockey game I've ever played, and my mind is focused anywhere but on the ice. I fuck up in the face-off and Montreal takes control of the puck, which leaves me racing down the ice. I catch Owen's gaze, and he's giving me a quizzical look.

Yeah, I know, man. I'm off my game tonight.

I huff out a deep exhale and get back to work, desperate to make a play before my shift is over.

I keep my head down and skate my ass off. Focusing on the game is the only thing that makes me feel semi-normal—with a crowd of thousands peering down at me from the stands. If I let myself think about the fact that these people have probably seen me naked, I'll end up cowering in the locker room.

The pace throughout the first period is fast and furious, and I'm happy to see my teammates are high-energy. Things were tense in the locker room before the game, like no one knew what to say to me. Well, there was one comment—and of course it came from Asher.

"Hey, movie star," he said in my direction when I strolled in.

"Fuck off, Asher," I grumbled.

"Who's your costar?" He grinned at me, like he was proud or something.

"None of your fucking business," I growled, meeting his eyes and daring him to push me further. "Got anything else to say to me?"

Taken aback, Asher raised his hands in surrender. "Understood. Chill, man."

After that, our captain, Grant, pulled me aside, and with his hand on my shoulder, assured me this would blow over soon, and just to keep my head in the game.

I nodded once, grunted again, and set about getting myself ready for the game, taping up my stick, putting on my pads, and doing all the shit I hoped would make me feel like a normal member of the team again. I didn't want to be an internet sensation. That was never my goal. I wanted to be known because of my skills on the ice, not because of my skills in the bedroom.

Hearing Asher ask about my costar pissed me off. No one needed to know, and so far, the public hasn't figured it out. The truth is, in our film debut, my body was mostly covering Sara's, and while I'm not an exhibitionist by any stretch of the imagination, if it means protecting her, I'm game. I don't give a shit who focuses on my ass instead of seeing Sara's face.

Locker-room drama aside, once we were on the ice, skating became as natural as breathing.

Now, in the face-off circle, I'm standing across from a guy named Sandersen. He's smirking at me, and I wait for whatever fucked-up comment he's going to lob my way.

"It's a wonder you can show your face here tonight. Half the world's seen that pathetic excuse you call a cock."

I keep my eyes on the ice, waiting for the puck to drop. "That's not what your mom said last night."

When the puck drops, I gain control and take it to the zone before it's snatched away. I approach the net and shoot, cursing when it goes wide. Sandersen checks me hard into the glass, but there's no call. After that play, things start to go south for us.

When Sandersen takes a whack at Owen, I check him hard in the ribs, just to make sure he knows he sure as hell isn't going to do that again. Even once the whistle blows, I keep on shoving, going back for a second helping. Eventually, the ref separates us, and I skate away with a scowl, my adrenaline still pumping hot.

At the start of the third, the game is tied 1–1. The moment we take the ice after the second intermission, everyone knows the entire third period will be intense.

Their team's top scorer fires at Owen and it's blocked, caught in his glove. At the next face-off, I seek redemption, ready to make something happen. Powering my way forward, I get a breakaway. I fling it over to Justin, who skates toward the net. Our line works incredibly well together, taking advantage of whatever opportunity is given.

It's shot and caught by their goalie, who rebounds it. Less than ten minutes remain in regulation time.

I skate toward the bench, and our second line is ready to take a shift. I grab a water bottle and watch the opposing team take a long-range shot.

Owen blocks the shot like his job depends on

it. And it does. Then he loses his stick, but Landon fetches it, and there's a traffic jam behind the net.

I watch in frustration, my chest still heaving. The team is off tonight—passing when they should be shooting, and shooting when they should be passing.

In the end, we lose 2–1, and I skate off the ice toward the locker room wearing a scowl and feeling majorly pissed off.

After my shower, I pull my phone out of my bag to find a text from Sara, and immediately my scowl eases.

`Are you going out tonight?`

Instead of answering right away, I jam my phone into my pocket and head out of the venue. Once I'm in the solitude of my car, I pull out my phone and dial her number.

"Hi," she says, answering after one ring. "Tough loss tonight."

"Yeah. I'm tired and frankly a little pissed off." I don't hide how I'm feeling from her.

"I get it. You played hard."

"But it wasn't enough," I mutter, unable to hide the anger and disappointment in my voice.

"Are you heading out with the guys?" she asks, and I don't miss the sense of hesitation in her voice.

"Nope, not tonight. I want to stay away from cameras and people's questions."

"Do you want some company? I could pick up your favorite ice cream."

"Yeah, come over?" I ask, my voice lifting hopefully as I pull out of the arena's private parking lot.

"I'll meet you there. See you soon."

It's a short ride to my place from the arena, and so I beat Sara by a couple of minutes. It's just enough time to turn on some lights before the intercom system buzzes to announce her arrival. When I open the front door, just the sight of her standing there in her jeans and oversized sweatshirt calms me.

A wry smile tugs at her lips as she takes me in. "You okay?"

"Better now that you're here." It's the truth. I step aside and let her in.

She smiles, patting me on the chest over my T-shirt, and then heads straight for my kitchen, where she begins unloading a plastic shopping bag onto the counter.

"For you." She hands me a plastic container, and I open it. Inside is a salmon Caesar salad, and my stomach immediately gives off a monstrous groan. "We'll save the ice cream for later."

"You're the best," I say with a grin, bending down to press a kiss to her cheek.

As nice as this is, I know better than to get used to it. With everything that's happened, there won't be any need to keep up the guise of our fake-dating. Somberly, I grab a fork and dig into my salad while Sara unpacks the rest of the containers.

When I finish, we sit side by side on the couch, and instead of waiting, we dig right into the ice cream. The creamy, sugary concoction lifts my mood the tiniest bit.

"What did you think of the game?" I ask, taking another bite.

She shrugs. "You guys looked good. You just got outplayed this time."

I nod. She's right. We did skate our asses off.

Our defense had some good plays, but we just couldn't make it happen. Some nights are like that.

Then she smiles like she's remembering something amusing. "God, did you see Becca in the stands?"

I shake my head. I never notice what's happening in the arena. Not the crazy songs or the kiss cam, none of it. My focus is one-hundred percent on the ice . . . well, unless Sara's in the crowd, and then it's more fifty-fifty.

"She used to be so calm and mild-mannered. Now anytime someone fires off a shot toward the net, she's on her feet screaming at them to get the fuck away from Owen."

I grin, chuckling softly. "I can't really picture Becca doing that."

"Yeah, if anyone approaches the crease, her voice goes up like eight octaves. It's bananas."

I try to imagine the buttoned-up Becca, assistant to the team owner, cursing out anyone who approaches the net. It's kind of an awesome mental image, honestly.

But my smile slowly fades as I watch Sara, because I suddenly want to know if she was screaming for me tonight. Somehow, I don't think so.

"You were extra tonight, weren't you?" She squints at me as if trying to read my emotional state.

It takes me a second to realize she's talking about the words I exchanged with Sandersen near the net. I'm sure it looked like little more than a childish shoving match.

"Eh. You don't fuck with our goalie. If you do, I'll fuck with you." She didn't need to know he also poked fun at our sex tape.

"Fair enough." She nods curtly.

I release a slow exhale and meet Sara's eyes. I'd give my left nut to know what she's really thinking. So far, all we've talked about is the hockey game.

"We should talk," she says, her tone measured.

I nod. It's true; we do need to. We haven't really spoken about everything that's happened since the video got leaked.

"I know, we should." *I'm just not ready to.* "But maybe not tonight."

She watches me, weighing my words. "Are you okay?"

“I will be. I’m just tired. Can we go to bed?” I want to hold her and snuggle her warm body close to mine, and pretend that everything is okay for a little while longer.

And thankfully, Sara lets me.

CHAPTER EIGHTEEN

Old News and New Beginnings

Sara

The beautiful thing about the internet is that although news may get out fast, it also gets old fast. And when I say fast, I mean six days. Because that's how long it took for all the sex tape madness to die down.

Six stressful days, mind you, but not even a full week has passed, and the hockey blogs are already moving on to the next victim.

This week's gossip? The power forward for Saint Louis got kicked out of a bar for doing a bit too much celebrating at a victory party. There's a video circulating and everything. But after a few days, he'll be old news too. Then it'll just be another fiasco with some other player. Hockey has no shortage of drama, that's for sure.

It's a Saturday night and I'm sitting on my couch, scrolling through the gossip sites while I wait for Teddy to pick me up. I told myself I wouldn't check these blogs anymore, but I have to know what's left in the press about Teddy now that the video has been down for a while.

Several minutes of scrolling, and the only evidence of our sex tape I can find is blurry screenshots of the video and a few blog posts with broken links to where the video used to be. I'll call that a success. Maybe I couldn't stop this thing from blowing up, but I kept it to a controlled burn instead of a blazing wildfire. Seems like a victory to me, even if it's a bittersweet one.

A good attorney knows how to take her victories where they come, and you really can't win them all. I'm mature enough to know that. We could have both been found out, both been fired from the careers we love.

My intercom rings, and I hop up from the couch to buzz Teddy up. He offered to give me a ride to poker night at Asher's tonight, and I couldn't turn down an opportunity for a few minutes alone with him before we see all our friends. Moments later, he's at my door, rocking a pair of ripped-up jeans and a leather jacket that has me practically drooling on my doormat.

"Hey there, stranger," I say, barely managing to keep my composure. "Are you ready for me to ruin your undefeated poker streak?"

Teddy laughs, but the look on his face is strained. "I'll believe it when I see it. Although I may be a little off my game tonight." He grips the back of his neck with one hand, his mouth pressing into a line instead of one of his usual lopsided grins, making me wonder what's going on. "This insane week has me carrying all my damn stress in my back and shoulders."

"Do you want me to rub your back for you?" I glance at my phone to check the time. "The chili dip I'm bringing still has a few more minutes in the oven, so we have a little time to kill."

Teddy lifts one brow at me, his mouth quirking up into the smile I've missed. "Really? You would do that?"

"Sure, what are fake girlfriends for?" I tease, but the second the words come out, I instantly regret saying them. Teddy and I haven't established where the two of us stand now that the threat of him losing sponsorships has died down and his team's PR department isn't breathing down his neck for a solution.

I pivot and head for the living room, avoiding eye contact and that whole conversation altogether. Based on the way he dodged that topic the other night, I'm not sure if he's ready to unpack it yet either. And what is there really to say . . . we have great sex together, sure, but aren't relationships built on a lot more than that?

While I grab a seat on the couch and get my back-rubbing hands ready, Teddy peels off his leather jacket, revealing a fitted forest-green V-neck that hugs his muscles and brings out the emerald in his eyes.

God, who gave him the right to be so damn good-looking? It's hardly fair.

I gesture toward the floor in front of me, doing my best not to stare, and Teddy takes a seat, his broad shoulders in line with my knees. I press my thumbs into the tight muscle between his neck and shoulders, kneading at the knots as I find them. And they're not hard to find. He was serious about carrying all of his stress here. A low groan of gratitude rumbles in his chest as my hands work across his back.

"Right there," he says. "Fuck, I needed this."

As he starts to relax under the pressure of my thumbs, I seize what might be one of our few moments alone tonight to ask one of the many tough questions bouncing around in my brain.

"Have you decided what you're going to do about your grandpa?"

Just asking the question puts a knot in my stomach. I know I'm not to blame for Denver withdrawing their interest in Teddy, but deep down, I feel partially guilty. If I could have kept that tape from leaking, he could be moving closer to his grandpa before the start of next season. Instead, that chance was snatched away.

"Not yet," he says, his voice low. "I'm going to fly down there after Wednesday's game to check in with him. I'll break the news then and float the idea of him moving here past him. It's going to be a really tough conversation."

My mind immediately jumps to my schedule for the upcoming week. Could I swing a trip to Denver on Wednesday night? Maybe Teddy could use a travel buddy. After everything he's told me about his grandpa, I would absolutely love to meet him. Plus, an extra persuasive voice might be helpful in convincing him that moving to Seattle is a great idea.

Then again, it's not my place to invite myself along on a trip like this. Meeting a man's grandfather is something reserved for a real girlfriend, not a fake one. If I'm even considered that anymore. I don't know what to think.

Are we still keeping up this charade? Or are we just friends again? Do friends give each other massages like this?

I shake the thought away, drawing my focus back to the tension in Teddy's shoulders. They teach you a lot of things in law school, but how to transition out of a fake relationship certainly isn't one of them.

"Sara? Are you okay?"

I must have spaced out for a second, because Teddy is looking up over his shoulder at me, his eyebrows knitted together.

"Um, yeah? Why?"

"Because you've been rubbing the same spot for, like, three minutes."

Flustered, I grasp at the quickest excuse I can find. "You had a really big knot there," I lie. *Nope. Definitely wasn't just overanalyzing everything about our relationship. No worries here.*

"Well, I think you got it." He laughs. "How much longer on the chili dip? I don't want to be the reason it burns."

"Four more minutes," I say, confirming with the timer on my phone. "Now turn back around. I'm not done with you."

The words leave a warm, buzzy feeling on my lips after I say them. *I'm not done with you.* I was just referring to the massage, but the thrumming of my heart in my throat tells me maybe I meant something more. Maybe I'm not done with Teddy King altogether.

As I push against his right shoulder, Teddy lets out a grunt of discomfort that sends me recoiling back. "You okay?"

"Fine," he says, his voice strained through clenched teeth. "That's just really, really tight right there. Go easy on it."

I try again, gentler this time, and he lets out a ragged sigh.

"You weren't kidding about being tense." I push the heel of my hand gently against his muscle, feeling it give beneath the pressure. "Maybe you should get in touch with the team's physical therapist and book some serious massage time."

Teddy shrugs, his muscles jumping beneath my thumbs. "Yeah. You're probably right." He pauses momentarily and chuckles, then adds, "But I prefer your hands on me to his. Thor wouldn't go this easy on me."

A flutter builds in my stomach. I want so badly to pull Teddy up onto the couch and on top of me, letting my hands cover a lot more ground than just his back. But is that what he wants? He was so hesitant to talk about this the other night, so why should tonight be any different?

And then I realize—tonight is *very* different.

The whole group is going to be at Asher's place tonight, and I have no idea how I'm supposed to act around Teddy. This conversation isn't just something I want to have. It's something we *need* to have. Pronto.

I suck in a deep breath and, summoning all the courage I have in me, ask the question of the evening.

"So, I guess we should probably tell our friends our secret tonight, huh?" I say, busying my fingers along the tense spots near his shoulder blades. "Break the news about this whole fake-dating thing and tell them it was just for the press?"

I hold my breath as I wait for his response, and beneath the pads of my fingers, I feel Teddy tense up the way I was expecting him to when I mentioned his grandpa.

"I guess," he mutters, but he doesn't sound very convincing, and his shoulders remain firmly pressed up against his ears.

An uncomfortable silence hangs between the two of us for a long moment before Teddy shrugs my hands off his shoulders and hops up on the couch next to me. His green eyes hit me with a look so sharp, it nearly knocks me over.

"But what if we didn't tell them?"

I scrunch my brows at him. "What do you mean? Just let them go on thinking that we're together?"

He shakes his head, laying one hand on my thigh. Even through my jeans, his touch sends a jolt of electricity through me.

"No, that's not what I mean." His voice is sincere with the tiniest bit of nervousness. He scrubs one hand through his dark hair, his gaze never breaking away from mine. "What I mean is that with all the shit I've dealt with these past few weeks, you've been the one bright spot in my life.

I don't want to let that go, Sara. I don't want to let *you* go."

"Do you mean . . ."

"I mean I want to ditch the 'fake' part of this fake-dating thing. And I want to keep doing this. For real this time."

Just as a smile starts to spread across my barely parted lips, my phone chimes. The timer. *Shit.* Worst timing ever.

Teddy smirks as I fumble with my phone. "So, uh, do you want to respond to that offer before or after you take the chili dip out?"

That gets a laugh out of both of us, but as for my response, how do you respond to a man who has just waved a magic wand and turned your fake relationship into a real one? Does the English language even have words appropriate for an occasion like this? What is there to say?

And then it hits me. There's nothing to say. All I can do is kiss him till he knows I accept.

CHAPTER NINETEEN

Biology Lessons

Teddy

Asher is hosting poker night at his place tonight. Pretty much everyone in our friend group is gathered here, either at the two poker tables that have been set up in the living room for tonight's festivities, or at the bar stools lining the kitchen island.

Sara and a couple of the girls—Bailey and Aubree—are in the kitchen talking. Becca is sitting on Owen's lap at one of the poker tables, and Elise is in the kitchen stirring something in a mixing bowl while she tells a story that has the other girls cracking up laughing.

A catering service has delivered various appetizers that are warming in aluminum chafing trays, and coolers of ice-cold beer are filled to the brim.

But I'm not interested in spicy chicken wings or chilled beverages right now—mostly because I haven't been able to pull my attention off Sara for long enough to focus on anything other than what a lucky bastard I am.

The guys are mostly seated at the poker tables, and we've just traded our cash for chips, ready for the night ahead of us. I'm at a table with Asher, Owen and Becca, Justin, and our rookie backup goalie, Morgan. Our team captain, Grant, and another rookie center named Landon sit at the other table, not quite ready to play yet, and they're discussing something in low tones.

"Rookie, get me another," Asher shouts to Morgan, shaking his empty beer bottle in his direction.

Morgan flips him the finger. "How long am I going to be a rookie?" he asks anyone in the room who seems to be listening to their exchange.

"It's your first season, bro. This is standard issue," Owen quips back. "My first year . . ." He pauses, his mouth lifted in a wry smirk. "Actually, I'm not allowed to talk about it. It's still a pending investigation. You know how serious management takes hazing nowadays."

Morgan's eyes widen slightly.

Owen is so full of shit. When he joined the lineup as our starting goalie, he had already spent a number of years playing for the minor affiliate team. The dude was highly respected for his skills in the net, and he took zero shit from anybody.

But that doesn't stop the concerned look that flashes across Becca's face. Owen leans down to whisper something in his fiancée's ear, and she visibly relaxes at whatever he's just said.

With a huff, Morgan hops up from his seat and grabs Asher's empty bottle. "Anyone else while I'm up?" he asks, heading toward the kitchen.

"I'll take one," Justin says.

Asher leans close, his elbows on the felt-lined table. "I just wanted him gone so you can tell us exactly how you managed to land a girl like Sara."

Owen grins, shifting Becca on his lap. "Yeah, was she drunk when she agreed to date you?"

Becca lightly slaps his shoulder, silently chastising him.

I shake my head, my smile unavoidable. "Laugh it up, boys. I know I hit the jackpot with her."

My gaze strays to the kitchen again, and I spot Sara hoisting herself up onto the counter near where Elise is still working, laughing about whatever they're discussing. Sara talks with her hands when she's excited, and her entire face lights up when she smiles.

God, she's beautiful. The guys are right. I still can't believe she's mine.

A hand claps down on my shoulder and squeezes. I blink and drag my attention away from Sara, and see that it's Asher.

"I'm just teasing, and you know I'm happy for you. But, seriously, when did this happen? The two of you . . . you've been scarce on details."

Maybe I should have grabbed one of those beers. I didn't expect an inquisition from my teammates tonight, but I guess on some level it makes sense. I haven't dated anyone in a couple of years now. The only meaningful relationship I've had is with my right hand. And, trust me, I plowed my way through lots of groupie attention.

My teammates don't know there was always a part of me yearning for more. They don't know that I actually love being in a relationship—love the movie nights on the couch and dinners at home, and waking up together on Saturday to do mundane errands like pushing a shopping cart through the aisles of a mega-store.

The idea that I've earned a shot to do all of that with Sara is mind-blowing. I can picture quiet afternoons at her place, taking her to dinner at one of our favorite chain restaurants and laughing the entire time. I can picture her meeting my grandpa Joe and making him smile. I can see a real future with her, and maybe that should scare me, but it just doesn't. Not even a little bit.

"We've been friends since college. You guys know that," I say on an exhale.

Several heads nod around the table.

"Well, back then, we were . . ." I clear my throat. ". . . casual for a little while. Then she went away for the summer and came back dating someone else. Figured I had lost my shot."

Becca frowns like the idea of that is the saddest thing she's ever heard.

"Over the years, I'd start dating someone, and then Sara would be single. And then by the time my relationship had run its course and I was single again, she'd have met someone. I guess this is the first time in forever that we were both single at the same time, and it was time to make my play."

“Aw,” Becca murmurs, watching me with rapt attention.

Here’s a weird thought: If I hadn’t been pushed by LaShonda, would we still be here?

Yes, I decide almost immediately. The words I’ve said to the guys are one-hundred percent true.

“That’s awesome, man,” Asher says, lifting his bottle.

I’m kind of surprised by his reaction. In all the years I’ve known him, I always assumed he was allergic to monogamy. But based on his reaction, he seems genuinely happy for me. For us.

Justin and Owen are grinning at me, and Becca looks so happy, she could burst.

“Morgan, get Teddy a beer,” Asher orders as soon as Morgan’s ass touches his seat.

With a groan, Morgan is up and moving toward the kitchen again while I chuckle.

After I’ve endured several hands of poker and lost sixty bucks, I push myself up from the table.

“You done?” Asher asks.

I nod. “Someone can take my spot.”

After I use the bathroom, I go to find Sara. She's seated at the other poker table, deep into a game herself, and I stand behind her, placing one hand on her shoulder, my thumb stroking the nape of her neck.

She tilts her chin, smiling up at me. "Hey."

"Hey, cutie."

There's a large stack of chips in front of her, and her hand is flush with face cards. The only players left in the game at this table are Sara and Grant.

I'm starting to wonder if there's anything she's not good at. Because so far, keeping her calm under pressure, showing resilience in the face of a scandal, and kicking ass at poker seem like the tip of the iceberg. Although we've known each other for years, we've only been dating for real for a couple of hours, and I love the fact that there's so much more I've yet to discover about her.

When Grant calls and they both reveal their hands, Sara lets out a little shout of happiness.

She's just won. Sliding all the chips from the center of the table toward her, she grins.

Grant mumbles, "Good game," and then pushes back from the table.

I chuckle, watching her count her winnings. "Nicely done, babe."

She gazes up at me, her blue eyes sparkling. "That was fun."

"Glad you enjoyed yourself." I lean down and place my lips at her temple.

"Is Grant, um, going to be mad at me now?"

"'Cause you just kicked his ass? No. He's normally a grumpy bastard. Don't let it bother you."

"I heard that," Grant calls from across the room, and I only chuckle.

"You ready to get out of here?" I ask.

Sara nods and slides up from the table, grabbing her stacks of chips. She cashes out with Asher, turning in the chips for some real green, and then we say our good-byes. I can't help but notice the curious glances our friends are casting in our direction as we head out, hand in hand.

I open the car door for Sara and watch her slide in. "Were the girls firing off questions about us while you were in the kitchen?"

"Not really, why?" I can hear the surprised smile in her voice.

I shrug. "The guys were. They wanted to know how a loser like me managed to snag a girl like you."

She turns to face me in the dimly lit interior of my car, her expression curious. "What'd you say?"

"That I'd knocked you up, and so you were stuck with me."

"TK!" She slaps my thigh playfully.

"Kidding, babe." I take her hand from my thigh and bring it to my lips where I kiss the back of it. "Maybe someday, though . . ."

Her gaze flashes to mine, and even though it's dark outside, I can see the heat in her eyes.

I didn't think I'd be ready for kids anytime soon, but it's not a mental image I'm hating, to be perfectly honest. Sara and me chasing after a little tyke, sharing warm looks and soft laughter. Sara and me making a home together . . . a family together.

"What did you really say?" she asks, pulling me out of my happy daydream.

"I actually told them that we'd dated casually back in college. Hope that was okay?"

She nods. “Yeah. I never really meant to hide it. I don’t know. I guess I just thought it was no one’s business but our own.”

“It wasn’t. But now that we’re together . . .”

“They kind of thought it came out of left field.”

“Exactly.” I nod. “But it didn’t. Not for me, anyway.”

We reach my building, and after scanning into the underground parking garage, I park in my designated parking spot and jog around to open Sara’s door.

“Thank you,” she murmurs.

Once inside, I waste no time in lifting her into my arms on the way to my bedroom. “You know you’re staying the night, right?” The words are whispered into the side of her neck.

She lets out a breathless little sigh, her fingers sliding into the hair at my nape. “Are you asking me, or telling me?”

“Overnights in my bed are reserved for girlfriends. No way I’m letting you go now that you’re mine.”

“Tonight or forever?”

“Let’s start with tonight. But that other word doesn’t scare me, just so you know.”

She exhales, and her mouth finds mine. “It doesn’t scare me either.”

Maybe it’s because I’ve known her for years. Maybe it’s because being friends first allowed us to build a strong foundation that couldn’t easily be torn down, or a level of trust that doesn’t normally exist in new relationships. But either way, I’m going for it, because my teammates were right. Sara is a catch, and I’m the luckiest dude in Seattle.

Once she’s stripped of her jeans and sweatshirt, my mouth is hot on hers as I guide her into the center of my bed. Sara works her hand into the front of my pants, and I let out a monstrous groan when the warmth of her palm closes around me, stroking firmly.

“Sweetheart.” I moan. “Need to be inside you.”

“Yes,” she says on an exhale as she begins clumsily trying to shove my jeans down over my hips.

With a chuckle, I decide to help her out, as entertaining as it is watching her efforts to de-pants me. Once I’m as bare as she is, Sara lets out a happy noise, running her palms along the expanse of my chest and abs, lingering over the flat discs of my nipples until I jolt with sensation.

"That better?" I ask.

"So much," she murmurs, her mouth pressing to mine.

We spend time on foreplay, but not much, because it seems she's just as eager for the main event as I am. But then something changes. Between the time it takes me to get her wet and ready for me, my fingers move from between her legs to give myself a stroke, I feel it. The air has shifted around us.

I gaze down at Sara, and even though it's mostly dark, I don't like what I see. Her eyes are filled with an emotion that's not easy for me to read. Anticipation. But also concern. Something is causing her to worry.

I pause, my mouth halfway to hers. "Tell me."

"Tell you what?" she says softly against my lips.

"What's going on inside that brilliant head of yours?"

She smiles and shakes her head. "Were you always this perceptive?"

"About certain things? Yes." Hockey, for one. I can read the game like it's written in stone. The girl I'm falling hard for? Absolutely. Other things? Not so much.

She shifts, lifting onto one elbow beside me and meets my eyes. "How will all this work?"

"Well, first I'm going to put my penis inside your—"

"Oh my God!" She stops me with a laugh, holding up one hand. "I don't need a ninth-grade biology lesson. I meant *us*. Your travel schedule. My hours that are only going to get more insane now that I've made partner. Your grandpa. All of it."

"We're going to make it work, babe."

"I know. But how? I need specifics."

I clear my throat, more than a little surprised to be having this conversation while we're both naked and seconds away from lots of . . . happy fun. But then again, I'm also not surprised, because this woman is thoughtful and articulate and likes to process information.

"Well, as for my grandpa, I'm planning to float the idea of moving him here the next time I see him. I don't know what he'll say, but I'd like him close by."

Sara nods once, watching me closely.

"Second, I will always support your career, so you never have to worry about that. As for how it will all work, you're going to move in here with me. That way, any downtime we both have will be spent together."

"That easy, huh?" she says with a raised brow.

"It could be." And I mean it.

I've never had this type of clarity before. Never felt so sure, so right about anything in my entire life. I first fell for this woman years ago; I just never thought I had a real shot with her.

"Teddy," she whispers, her lips finding mine in a sweet kiss.

"I want you here, babe. Whenever you're ready. Which I hope is soon. We've waited long enough."

She swallows, nodding. "I think you're going to be really good at this boyfriend thing."

"I will rock the shit out of this boyfriend thing," I say smugly.

Sara smiles, biting her lip as she watches me. "Now, about that biology lesson . . ."

I trace my fingertips lightly along her skin and feel her shiver at my touch. "Here, let me show you how it's done."

• • •

The following morning, Sara has left for a workout at the gym, and I'm sitting in my study waiting for a phone call from the head of the Ice Hawks that my agent said is coming this morning.

My agent has been pushing Seattle to get me a contract, either so I can accept it and know for sure I'm staying here, or so we can use it as a basis point for my value when we negotiate with other teams. My stomach is in a knot, and the cup of coffee I shared with Sara is churning inside me now. I wish she hadn't left.

My cell rings, flashing a number I don't have programmed in, and I grab it from the desk. "Hel-lo? This is Teddy."

"Mr. King." The deep cheerful voice belongs to our team's current owner, Bryce O'Malley. "Thanks for making time this morning."

"Of course, sir."

I'm really not sure if I'm supposed to make small talk, or say something interesting about the team, or ask about his kids. But thankfully, I'm saved from awkward silence by the sound of O'Malley clearing his throat.

"Let me cut to the chase. Your agent is going to call you in a little while and present you with an offer. We've worked hard on cutting you a great deal, and I hope you'll be pleased, but that's not why I'm calling."

"Oh," is the inarticulate thing that falls out of my mouth. "It's not?"

"No, son. It's not. I wanted to let you know, personally, that I want you on this team."

"I—thank you, sir."

He makes a noise of agreement. "I could tell you a bunch of fancy things about your leadership on the ice, your puck-management skills, the stats you've racked up that the sports analysts are happy about. But the truth is, I like you, Teddy. I like how you conduct yourself, and I thought how you handled that whole fiasco recently was pretty admirable. LaShonda in PR had a lot of positive things to say about you too. I think you set a good example for the younger guys. I think you're just hitting your prime, and I want you to be in Seattle when that happens. I hope you'll accept our offer."

It would help if I knew what the heck the offer is. But my agent let it slip that they were talking in the tens of millions over the course of a four-year contract.

"Thank you, sir. I appreciate that. And I want to formally apologize for any negative press I brought down on the team."

"Ah . . ." He makes a noise like he's waving off my apology. "Shit happens, son."

I almost choke on a laugh but manage to restrain myself. "Um. True. I guess it does."

"Well, we'll talk soon," he says before ending the call.

After I hang up, I stare down at my phone, my emotions running all over the place. It feels like my future is in Seattle.

But what about my past?

CHAPTER TWENTY

Date Night

Sara

The last week of my life has been an absolute whirlwind, to say the least.

Between Teddy and me becoming an official couple, my case overload at work, and the uncertainty of his next career move, I've been feeling on edge. But all of that changed the second Teddy put pen to paper and signed a contract, accepting a new four-year extension to play for the Seattle Ice Hawks.

Work will always be busy, and life will always find a way to throw us curveballs, but at least now I know I'll be fielding said curveballs with my ridiculously hot and incredibly sweet boyfriend by my side.

Every time I say *boyfriend*, I start smiling like

a teenage girl who's just been told her crush likes her. It also feels damn good knowing that he's not about to move across the country when we've only just gotten serious.

And while all of Seattle is buzzing about their hockey franchise hanging on to the strongest forward they've had in decades, I'm busy daydreaming about our future together here in Seattle. I don't want to take things too quickly, but that hasn't stopped my imagination from conjuring up images of coming home to Teddy's swanky apartment every night, the two of us cooking dinner and snuggling up with peanut butter ice cream and a movie on the weekends.

During hockey season, when he's traveling from city to city for away games, I can picture myself curled up on the couch with a book and a glass of wine when he walks in the door, drops his duffel on the floor, and scoops me into his arms. I want to be what he comes home to.

It all seems so simple, boring and domestic, but it makes my heart beat faster—maybe because I've lived alone for so long and I'm finally ready to have someone to share my life with.

These are the daydreams that have been helping me pass the time at my desk while I wait for

Teddy to get home from his Denver trip.

Immediately following the press conference announcing his contract extension, where I turned every shade of pink as he thanked his girlfriend for supporting him along the way, Teddy and I hopped in the back of a town car to drop him at the airport. And so began the longest three days of my life. I feel a little silly about missing him while he's away on such a short trip, but the conversation we had on our way to the airport is enough to get me through.

"It's just three days, babe," Teddy reminded me, pulling me as close to him as my seat belt would allow. "What's three days when I just signed on to be all yours for the next four years?"

"You signed on to play for the Ice Hawks for four years," I said. "Where in that contract exactly did it say that you were required to be my boyfriend that whole time? I'm not sure of the legality of that. The lawyer in me can spot all kinds of loopholes."

I'll never forget the deep, rumbling sound of his laugh as he laced his fingers with mine. "After all these years, I've finally got you for real, Sara. Four years is just the beginning. I'm not ever letting you go."

Between reliving that moment repeatedly and

working overtime on my caseload to pass the time, I've kept plenty busy during Teddy's time away. I know how important this visit is to him—he has just a few days to either talk his grandpa into relocating or to accept the fact that he'll be all right in Denver, so I'm trying not to take up too much of his time with constant texts or phone calls.

But the few text conversations we've had have been nothing short of over-the-top cute. Teddy's spent the last few days bragging that he's planned the perfect night for the two of us for when he gets back, but he refuses to spill the details.

I've been pretending to be annoyed about it, but in reality, my stomach is filled with butterflies at the thought of what he might have planned. I can't believe this is my life. My college hookup turned fake boyfriend turned *real* boyfriend has a cute date planned for the two of us, and I'm giddy at the thought and counting down the seconds until his plane lands back in Seattle.

The day before Teddy's flight home, I'm settled at my desk with my laptop open, and I double-click on my video-chat app and listen as it starts ringing. As soon as we became official, Teddy asked that we schedule some time during his Denver trip for me to unofficially meet Grandpa Joe. Teddy has a game tonight in Denver, which is probably the only reason his coach agreed to let him go in the first place.

There's a giddy feeling in my stomach as the phone rings, waiting for Teddy to accept my video call. It means so much to me that he wants Grandpa Joe, the most important person in his life, to meet me, even if it is just via webcam for now.

My laptop makes an echoey dinging sound as Teddy's face pops up on my screen, a cheesy smile on his face. God, that smile. One look at him, and I can't help but smile too.

"Hey, babe, I miss you," Teddy says softly, the smile never leaving his face.

"I miss you too."

A soft chuckle comes from beside Teddy, from who I assume is Grandpa Joe. "Are you going to introduce me to your girl, or what?"

Teddy shakes his head. "Sara," he says, pivoting the camera to show a second face. "Meet Grandpa Joe."

My smile doubles in size. Grandpa Joe has wrinkles around his eyes and a shock of thick white hair. One look at him, and it's no mystery where

Teddy got his height. They make an adorable sight sitting side by side on a brown couch, and I have a strange moment where my throat gets tight.

"So this is the woman my grandson can't stop talking about," Grandpa Joe says with a smile that matches Teddy's. "It's nice to meet you, little lady."

I chuckle and nod. "Thank you. It's so nice to meet you too. Are you two having a nice visit?"

Teddy looks at his grandpa with a wry smile. "We're staying out of trouble. For the most part."

It sounds like there's a story there—one I hope to find out later. Maybe when Teddy calls me tonight as he's done every night to tuck me into bed with a story from their day. It's always something mundane, like grocery shopping or a pharmacy visit, but he always manages to make me laugh.

After a few minutes of conversation, it's as clear as day where Teddy picked up a bit of his stubborn streak. Because as friendly as Grandpa Joe is, he's also adamant about not relocating to Seattle. It's the primary topic of conversation throughout our call, and I get the impression that it's been one of the only things discussed between the two of them over the past few days of Teddy's visit.

"I can't give up and stop living simply because

my grandson is worried." Grandpa Joe frowns, folding his arms over his chest. And to be honest, he has some good points.

As he gushes about how much he loves his community center, his church, and throws in the detail of a cute nurse that seems to have caught his eye, I admit that I might be a little convinced that maybe Grandpa Joe is in the right place after all.

The look on Teddy's face tells me that it's not what he wanted to hear, but there's something about his eyes that's a bit different from the other times he's talked about Grandpa Joe. A spark of hope is there that wasn't there before. Maybe, like me, he's a little convinced too.

As the call wraps up, I manage to mediate a reasonable agreement that Teddy will fly down to Denver more often in the off season, and that Grandpa Joe will come and visit us in Seattle.

His grandpa seems a little grumpy about how infrequently he sees Teddy during hockey season, but when I chime in with the idea that Teddy could get him and that cute nurse free tickets to the games in Denver, his attitude shifts for the better.

When we say our good-byes, Grandpa Joe makes me promise through a virtual pinkie swear that I'll join Teddy the next time he visits. As I hold up my pinkie to my laptop, I see Teddy grinning like a fool in the corner of my screen. It sends a warm tingle through me as I remember the time I stopped myself from offering to join Teddy on his Denver trip. I thought that was something reserved for real, serious girlfriends only.

But now that's what I am. Teddy's real, serious girlfriend. Who really, seriously can't wait for him to get back to Seattle.

Luckily, I don't have to wait too much longer. Teddy's flight touches down late after the game tonight, but since I have an early morning work meeting, I won't see him until after work tomorrow.

• • •

All day Teddy's been texting, and I've been antsy at my desk, watching the minutes tick by, slowly getting closer to the time I can leave and get to him.

At five o'clock on the nose, I rush home and ditch my corporate pantsuit, shaking my high pony down into loose, natural waves. I've spent all week wondering what on earth Teddy could have planned for this evening that's worth making such a big deal about. Even though he refused to give me any details, he did give me two very important instructions: dress to impress and come hungry.

My flirty pink strappy dress and black stilettos fit the bill nicely, and since I worked through lunch, I'm absolutely starving. Now all I need is the third crucial component of this date night— my date. I'm just finishing up refreshing my makeup when the intercom buzzes, sending my stomach jumping for joy and my feet racing across the apartment to let him in.

I swing open the door and am greeted by a man who could have practically invented the term "drop-dead gorgeous." Because for a moment, I just stand there like I've forgotten how to breathe, bowled over by how handsome he is. Teddy is rocking a fitted charcoal-gray suit and a navy tie, his hair neatly combed back, and has a dozen red roses in his hand.

My lips part and a tiny gasp escapes me, which makes him chuckle.

"Honey, I'm home," he jokes, then moves to hand the roses to me.

But it isn't the roses that catch my eye. Screw the flowers. I'll take the man who's holding them.

I weave my fingers behind his neck and push up onto my tiptoes until our lips meet in a long, tender kiss that's well worth the three days of waiting. When I finally pull back, a devilish smile spreads across his lips, making me want to kiss them all over again.

"Well, hello to you too," he teases as I tug him into the apartment. "Miss me?"

"Like crazy," I admit on a laugh. "But now I don't have to."

Once we've freed up his hands by finding a vase for that gorgeous bouquet, we spend a few more minutes catching up on all the kissing we've missed out on over the past few days. I think I would forgo just about any date to stay here in his arms all night, but the grumble in my stomach that interrupts us mid-makeout session says otherwise.

"Isn't it normally my job to interrupt our sexy time by being too hungry?" he says with a laugh.

I shrug, placing one hand on my stomach as if it will silence the grumbling. "I skipped lunch because you told me to come hungry."

"I also told you to dress to impress." His eyes trace my curves, lingering at the places where the pink fabric clings extra tight to my figure. "You sure do follow instructions well. And as much as I hate myself for saying this, can the make-out session wait just a little longer? I've got a car waiting so we don't miss our reservation."

"Hmm, as long as our next make-out session leads to us being naked."

"Babe, that's a given."

In the back of the town car, I sit on my hands to keep them off Teddy. That suit hugs his muscular chest and arms in all the most delicious ways, but now isn't the time to tear him out of it. Not when, apparently, we have reservations somewhere swanky.

"Will you tell me where we're going now?" I plead, jutting out my bottom lip for effect and giving him the best puppy-dog eyes I can muster.

He laughs and shakes his head. "Being cute isn't going to work, babe. Let's just say we're going somewhere we both love."

When the car finally pulls into the parking lot, my jaw nearly hits the floor as I spot the big, glowing red pepper outside my window.

"Oh my God. Chili's! We're going to Chili's?" I shriek, twisting in my seat to face him.

Teddy's grin takes up nearly his whole face. "Is that okay with you?"

I love that he remembered this detail—that I admitted my love for chain restaurants on our very first date—and this restaurant in particular.

"Uh, yes! This is perfect." I lean over and kiss him hard. "Best date ever."

I love that even though we could afford someplace much nicer, and splurge on a bottle of wine that costs several hundred dollars—tonight we're going for comfort and familiarity.

That's what Teddy is, I realize . . . my safe space, my comfort zone, all the good and happy things in life. There's nothing stuffy or pretentious about him. I don't have to work hard to impress him or walk around on eggshells. I can just relax and be myself. It's literally the best feeling in the world.

"It's only just starting," he murmurs against my lips before hopping out of the car and racing around to open my door for me. "Shall we, mademoiselle?" he asks, offering me his hand.

Eagerly, I place my hand in his, my smile growing by the second. We walk toward the restaurant hand in hand, but I stop him before he has a chance to pull the oversized wooden doors open.

"Should we be thinking about cameras? If you

used your name on the reservation, some waiter might have spilled the beans to the press that you're going to be here."

Teddy shakes his head, squeezing my hand extra tight. "Who cares? We're not doing this for the cameras anymore. We're doing this for us. And if someone happens to leak a picture to some hockey blog, there's no one else I'd rather be caught on camera with than my sexy-as-hell girlfriend."

After leaving a slow, sweet kiss on my lips for reassurance, he pulls open the door and we walk in, by far the most overdressed couple to ever enter a restaurant this casual. After giving the hostess Teddy's name, we're led to a table toward the back, and I can feel eyes following us. I don't know whether it's because of Teddy or because we're dressed so fancy. It's probably a bit of both. We take our place at our reserved red vinyl booth, and I'm still smiling big.

"If I knew all I had to do to get that kind of smile out of you was bring you to Chili's, I would have asked you on a date years ago."

My heart stutters at the thought of what could have been, but I keep my expression neutral. Still, I can't help but ask, "Why didn't you?"

He leans over, linking his fingers with mine. "I wanted to. Shit, I *really* wanted to. But both of our careers were taking off, and I was immature and doing stupid shit . . ."

"You can say you were screwing puck bunnies."

He shakes his head, a wry grin spreading over his face. "Yeah, you kinda had a front-row seat to that, didn't you?"

"It doesn't bother me. I gave you enough shit about it back then anyway."

It's true. Every time I saw him hooking up or on the way to hooking up, I'd call him out. Did I wish it had been me he was hooking up with? Yeah, but he was a hot, young professional hockey player. Women threw themselves at him, literally. I was in a long-term relationship with my career, so timing wasn't on our side.

"But, yeah," Teddy says, his eyes locking on mine. "I wanted you, but I didn't just want you for a night, or a week, or a month. Every time I looked at you, I saw forever, and I didn't wanna fuck that up by pursuing you when I knew we both weren't there yet. And just so you know, I was planning on making my move, long before the tape scandal hit, so don't think that's the only reason we're sitting here now."

I look at our fingers as heat hits my cheeks. "What moves would you have made?"

"Whatever I did to win you over in college, I would have done all of that times a thousand. I would make you laugh because I know you love to laugh. I would have sent your favorite ice cream to the office when I knew you were working late. I would have put myself in front of you as much as I could have. I wouldn't have stopped until I'd won your heart, and I wouldn't have been happy until you were in my arms."

A waitress wanting to take our drink orders interrupts us, and after she leaves, I meet Teddy's eyes and smile, loving that he's giving me the same fond look. I could literally stare at him forever and never get enough. He's so incredibly handsome, and I love that he just bared his soul to me.

The idea of moving in with him hasn't left my mind since he told me that us living together was what he wanted. The truth is I want that too.

The idea of waking up next to him and falling asleep wrapped around his body is one of the many things I want. I want us to cook together, to snuggle on the couch, to do mundane tasks like grocery shopping, paying bills, having friends over for dinner parties, and being lazy together on Sundays. I want every part of my life to mesh with his. The exciting, the boring, the normal, and the extraordinary.

"We're going to need a freezer fully stocked with ice cream at all times," I tell him in my lawyer voice. "Sharing the remote is nonnegotiable, and you can't complain when I want to watch back-to-back chick flicks. Oh, and sleeping naked is a must. No compromise on that one."

"Hmm, I think I can agree to your terms. I have a few of my own, though."

His eyes flash with mischief, and I brace myself.

"Naked breakfasts every Sunday, filthy phone sex when I'm on the road, and I'm going to need you to give me regular massages because, babe, that massage was freaking perfection. Oh, one more. Date nights every chance we get, even when we're old and have a bunch of kids."

He locks his eyes with mine when he mentions kids. We're new in this relationship, but it feels like we've been moving toward this exact moment for years.

I wait for fear and anxiety to set in, to start freaking out, but none of it hits me. All I feel is warmth, love, and excitement. I imagine Teddy with a little girl curled up against his chest, and a little boy following him around everywhere. I visualize Christmas mornings, the first day of school, and the two of us negotiating over baby names. I want every single thing he's offering.

"You with kids is an entertaining thought," I finally say. "Our little girl is going to have you wrapped around her little finger. Imagine what you'll be like when she starts dating."

His response is immediate. "She won't be allowed to date."

I giggle and lean over the table to kiss him softly. "Your baby girl is going to have a mom who's a lawyer, so she'll know how to talk her way out of anything, and she'll probably inherit your stubborn streak. So, TK, you've got no chance."

"Fuck." He groans. "Boys. We're only having boys."

I sit back in my seat and watch as his expression softens.

"So, do you agree to my terms?" he asks before he lifts his iced tea to his lips after the waitress places our drinks between us.

"Hmm, being naked with you, hearing your voice be all husky when you're horny, having my hands on you, and seeing you become a DILF? They are tough terms to agree to." I lick my lips, and his eyes zone in. "Throw in eating Chili's in bed, and you've got yourself a deal."

His gorgeous lips lift into a smile that reaches his eyes and takes over his entire face. "We're doing this? You're moving in, and we're making my place our home?"

I nod, excitement bubbling within me. "Yeah, we're doing this."

"We're starting right now." He lifts his hand and signals for the waitress to come over.

I have no clue exactly what we're starting. But when the waitress reaches our booth, I find out exactly what he means.

"Can we place our order to go? We won't need our table any longer."

I bite my lip to stop myself from laughing.

Teddy looks at me expectantly from across the

table and raises his eyebrows as he nods down at the menu in front of me. After I order wings and a burger and fries, and Teddy orders what seems like half of the menu, the waitress rushes back to the kitchen.

"I feel like I'm going to fall in love with you a little more tonight."

"Get ready, Dawson, because I plan on making you fall in love with me a little more every single day." He finishes the rest of his iced tea and pushes the empty glass to the edge of the table.

After finishing my soda, I put my glass next to his. "You're playing your cards right, King."

"So, Chili's and my cock is all it takes?" He pretends to write something on an imaginary piece of paper. "Noted."

I snort, shaking my head. "Don't forget the ice cream waiting for us in the freezer. Chili's, ice cream, and your cock. In that order."

He scoffs. "You are such a liar."

After our food arrives packaged neatly in some to-go containers, Teddy slides out from his side of the booth and grabs my hand. I smile as he pulls me out of the restaurant and into the waiting town car. On the way back to his place—no, wait, *our* place—I can't resist opening the appetizer container and eating a chicken wing. When I moan, I feel Teddy's eyes lock on me. I make a point to moan a little longer, and I smirk when he shifts beside me.

He leans in, his warm breath curling around my ear. "Clothes off as soon as we get home."

"Tonight keeps getting better and better." I lift my fingers to his lips.

He licks the sauce off slowly, and instantly heat flashes between my thighs.

We're barely inside the doorway before Teddy sets down the bags of takeout and his mouth is on mine—leaving hot, urgent kisses.

"Get over here." He hauls me closer with a breathy murmur, and I move willingly into his arms. "Did I tell you how much I missed you?"

I shake my head. "Why don't you show me?"

"Gladly, babe."

Inside the kitchen, he places me roughly on the counter and steps between my thighs. I'm torn between wanting to move this party into the bedroom, or staying right where we are, because I can't imagine pulling my mouth away from his long enough to walk down the hallway.

"Babe." He groans when I reach between us and begin unbuckling his belt.

His hands are in my hair and his lush mouth is fused to mine while my hands do very naughty things to his perfect manhood.

The deep rumbling in his throat tells me that my efforts are appreciated. But when Teddy begins stripping me right there in the kitchen, it's game over.

I want him here. Now. Forever.

This is how we end up having hot, frantic sex on his kitchen counter. The man's stamina is incredible. He only lets go after he's wrung two orgasms from my pliant body as I cling to his powerful shoulders. It's intense and perfect. Just like everything else with him.

After I clean up and pull on one of Teddy's discarded T-shirts, I climb in bed next to him, smiling as he begins laying out our food and making it look like an epic bed picnic. Our dinner may not be as hot as it should be, the fries may be soggy, and the burger won't taste as great as it would freshly cooked, but I don't give a shit.

I have my man. We're in our bed, in our home. We've talked about the future, and I have images of Teddy as the father of my children on constant rotation in my head. Oh, and let's not forget that I'm surrounded by our favorite food, and I've just had ridiculously hot sex.

I couldn't want or need anything else.

"Best date ever," I whisper.

He leans in until he is all I can see. "Today's the first day of the rest of our lives. You ready for that?"

I smile. "Oh, I am so ready."

"That's my girl."

And I am. I'm his. Finally.

Today, tomorrow, next week, and forever.

EPILOGUE

Teddy

"This is humiliating." I groan, trying to conceal my junk behind a hockey puck.

I know what you're thinking—*what the hell?* And yeah, you'd be right. This situation is all kinds of messed up.

"Don't be a baby. It's for charity," Asher says, giving me a mocking look.

I give him a dark look and flip him the middle finger. "Just wait till it's your turn, fucker."

We've all been brought here today—a drafty warehouse on the outskirts of the city, which isn't the best place to get naked as far as I'm concerned—under the guise of it being "for a good cause."

I'm getting really tired of hearing those words

leave our friend Aubree's mouth. And considering she's not even here today, what the actual hell? I know she works for the charity that the team supports, but this is getting a little ridiculous.

Actually, *little* is the wrong word entirely, because if the photographer seriously expects me to fit my junk behind a five-ounce rubber disk, he's insane.

I called Sara thirty minutes ago when I learned about his "creative vision" for the photo shoot, and asked her to come up here and make sure I don't disgrace myself, because I really don't want to be the face of yet another messed-up scandal. The world has seen its fair share of my cock already, so I want to keep it under wraps. Can you really blame me?

I hear a commotion in the other room, the sound of a metal door closing, and then Sara's sweet laughter echoes through the warehouse.

She's here, thank fuck.

Sara walks toward us with Bailey in tow behind her. They've been out this afternoon having lunch and getting their nails done. When I called in desperation, they were finishing up, so they said they'd come straight away. Seriously, I have the best girlfriend in the world.

They're dressed similarly, both sporting jeans and ponytails. Sara smirks at me and shakes her head. Poor Bailey doesn't know where to look, her eyes widening almost comically as she takes in the scene.

I groan when Sara reaches me. "Thank God you're here."

Sara pauses in front of me, her eyes dropping from mine to the hockey puck I'm holding in front of my crotch, giving me a questioning look as if to ask, *What the hell have you gotten yourself into now?*

"*I know. Help me.*" I mouth the words to her in desperation.

Sara laughs, and although I want to be annoyed by the fact that she finds my predicament funny, instead I'm instantly calmed by the warm sound of her laughter.

"Where's Aubree?" is the first thing out of her mouth.

"That's a great question," Asher mutters from beside me.

"And one we don't have the answer to," I say

helpfully.

"Okay, hang tight, guys. I'm going to fix this. Oh, and TK, do not move that puck. I don't want people seeing what's mine," Sara says before she struts over to where the photographer is adjusting a cloth backdrop and his lighting.

"What's she doing?" Asher asks, all of our eyes on my girlfriend as she moves in close to the unsuspecting photographer.

"Going into full-blown lawyer mode," Bailey says, answering for me.

"That's so fucking hot," Asher says on a sigh.

"Yeah, it is." I agree, my eyes still on my girl from across the room, where she's now animatedly talking with her hands to the photographer.

"This can't be what Aubree intended for today," Bailey says.

I don't know the tiny five-foot, one-inch brunette well, although I've gotten to know her a little better since Sara and I started officially dating two months ago, because they hang out often. I know Bailey's been in med school for the last few years and is close to graduating, and that she's ridiculously smart and feisty, so her personality meshes well with Sara's.

Before either Asher or I can answer, Bailey whips out her phone. "You can get dressed if you want." She motions toward us with a dismissive wave. "This might take a few minutes to get sorted, but Sara will get it done."

Nodding, I turn my back to her, drop the puck, and tug on my discarded athletic shorts. "Roger that."

Asher is dressed only in a pair of padded hockey pants, which are, of course, shorts, with the laces in front undone.

Morgan and Landon are here too, awaiting their turns across the room in some metal folding chairs. They're passing the time by playing on their phones, oblivious to the drama unfolding.

I find it interesting that Owen and Justin got out of coming today, and I can't help but think maybe their women sensed this would be a clusterfuck and called a penalty. It's not outside the realm of possibility.

On the phone beside us, Bailey recounts the situation to Aubree. "This can't be what you intended." Her eyes widen as she listens, and then a second later, she disconnects the call, just as Sara is strolling back from her lively talk with the photographer.

"Okay, I guess it is what she intended. Apparently, photos of naked athletes are guaranteed to sell a lot of calendars for charity," Bailey says, glancing at Asher.

Sara's expression is stern. "Well, I think the public has seen enough of my man's private business. His abs will sell calendars just fine as far as I'm concerned."

Relief washes through me. She's totally right. As usual.

But Sara's not done. "I spoke with the photographer, and you guys are free to pose in whatever you're most comfortable wearing. If that's your birthday suit, so be it, but if it's not, the choice is yours, gentlemen."

Asher grins. "Yo, rookies," he calls out, and Morgan and Landon both lift their heads from their phones. "This applies to you too."

For a second, I think maybe they're about to ask us what's going on, but Landon salutes us with a thumbs-up, and Morgan nods.

"Awesome. Because my manscaping is nowhere near as on point as TK's," Landon calls out.

Morgan only smirks before going back to whatever has him so entertained on his phone.

An easy peal of laughter slips from Bailey's lips. Then she widens her eyes and mouths toward me, "*Sorry*."

Apology accepted.

"Seriously, dude," Asher says, gesturing toward my crotch. "Ten points for having excellent manscaping."

"Seriously, would you fuck off?" I grumble as I tug Sara toward me and wrap my arm around her waist.

"That's fair. Your lawyer girlfriend just got us off the front-page news. Which I appreciate wholeheartedly," he says with a nod. "So, yes, I will kindly fuck off. For now."

Damn straight. My *hot* lawyer girlfriend, I mentally add.

"Are you going to stick around while I get this done?" I ask Sara softly.

She looks up at me and nods. "Of course. Go and show them how hot my boyfriend is."

Fuck, I love hearing her call me her boyfriend. I lean down and kiss her quickly before heading toward the photographer to get this done so we can get out of here.

After I'm photographed in nothing but a pair of black athletic shorts, it's Asher's turn. And when Bailey volunteers to rub oil all over his abs, her face goes as red as a tomato. Gone is the normally confident girl with an easy comeback for any situation.

Sara and I exchange a curious look as I tug my Ice Hawks sweatshirt back over my head.

"You think something could be going on with Bailey and Asher?" I ask, still watching them.

"No," Sara says too quickly. "Bailey would *never* date a hockey player."

"Never?" I ask. And if I sound skeptical, it's because I am. Hockey players are awesome. Duh.

"Never," she says again.

"Kinda sounds like someone I once knew." I give Sara a smirk, and she laughs. "Thanks for coming to my rescue today," I say, lifting her chin so I can meet her eyes.

"Anytime, handsome."

I lower my lips to hers, kissing her softly, briefly, before retreating. "You're the best." My hands drift from her waist down to her ass, where I give it a firm squeeze.

"Behave," she says, her eyes flashing with her desire. "I might have told the photographer I was the team's attorney, and you're totally going to blow my cover."

I chuckle. "Wouldn't want to do that."

"Exactly," she says, her eyes lifting to mine with a mischievous look.

We're interrupted by the sound of Bailey gasping for air as her laughter floats through the air. Asher is cracking up next to her, and she's clutching his bicep while doubled over.

Okay, what the hell is going on with these two?

"You sure she's not interested in him?" I ask, cocking a brow at Sara.

"Positive," she says without hesitation.

"Care to place a bet on that?"

She grins, raising her eyebrows. "How much are we talking, Mister Twelve-million-dollar Contract?"

For a moment, I'm stunned into silence, because Sara and I never talk about money. I guess we don't need to—we both make plenty of it. "As my lawyer, you know I can't comment on that."

She laughs, a deep throaty sound that makes my entire body ache for her.

Leaning down, I whisper near her ear, "That lawyer act you pulled earlier was totally sexy, by the way. All I'm thinking about now is bending you over that chair and plowing into you until you're moaning my name and coming around my cock."

"Promises, promises," she murmurs, staring at me with lust-filled eyes.

"It's game time when we get home, babe. You and me."

Sara smiles at me, her expression softening, and my entire body relaxes.

God, I love this girl.

I scored big-time when Sara agreed to be mine. I could score a thousand goals on the ice, but none of them will ever compare to scoring the biggest goal of my life—my sexy-as-hell, fierce partner in crime. I've said it once and I'll continue saying it: I'm the luckiest bastard in the world.

• • •

I hope you enjoyed reading Trying to Score! Up next is Asher and Bailey's story in ***Crossing the Line.***

Check out a little sneak preview on the next page.

HOT JOCKS 4

CROSSING THE LINE

Hello, rock? Meet hard place.

Recovering from a pulled groin muscle isn't exactly how I planned to spend my much-needed summer vacation.

But I'll admit, being nursed back to health by my gorgeous friend Bailey, who's just graduated from medical school, doesn't exactly sound like a hardship.

We spend a week together at my family's beach house, a week of swimming and barbecues, a week of entertaining my little cousins and sleeping right across the hall from each other. A week of watching Bailey grow closer with my mom and sisters, and my wacky but lovable grandma. A week of enjoying Bailey tending to me—which is saying something, because it involves a lot of shoving ice packs into my underwear and taping up sore muscles.

She's funny and kind, and after just being myself for the first time in a long time, I find my walls come tumbling down. But when Bailey says she's not looking for a relationship, I'm bound and determined to be more than just the fun hookup who sprained his groin a second time—this time with her.

Get Your Copy of *Crossing the Line* at

kendallryanbooks.com/books/crossing-the-line

Acknowledgments

I'll keep this short and sweet. Thank you to my entire team. It takes a village to write and release a novel, and I'm so thankful for each of you. And next … I would like to thank my lovely readers for continually trusting me to deliver a satisfying read. Thank you, thank you, *thank you*! I hope I never let you down.

Get Two Free Books

Sign up for my newsletter and I'll automatically send you two free books.

www.kendallryanbooks.com/newsletter

Follow Kendall

Website

www.kendallryanbooks.com

Facebook

www.facebook.com/kendallryanbooks

Twitter

www.twitter.com/kendallryan1

Instagram

www.instagram.com/kendallryan1

Newsletter

www.kendallryanbooks.com/newsletter

About the Author

A *New York Times*, *Wall Street Journal*, and *USA TODAY* bestselling author of more than two dozen titles, Kendall Ryan has sold over two million books, and her books have been translated into several languages in countries around the world. Her books have also appeared on the *New York Times* and *USA TODAY* bestseller list more than three dozen times. Kendall has been featured in publications such as *USA TODAY*, *Newsweek*, and *In Touch Magazine*. She lives in Texas with her husband and two sons.

To be notified of new releases or sales, join Kendall's private Mailing List.

www.kendallryanbooks.com/newsletter

Get even more of the inside scoop when you join Kendall's private Facebook group, Kendall's Kinky Cuties:

www.facebook.com/groups/kendallskinkycuties

Other Books by Kendall Ryan

Unravel Me
Filthy Beautiful Lies Series
The Room Mate
The Play Mate
The House Mate
The Impact of You
Screwed
The Fix Up
Dirty Little Secret
xo, Zach
Baby Daddy
Tempting Little Tease
Bro Code
Love Machine
Flirting with Forever
Dear Jane
Finding Alexei
Boyfriend for Hire
The Two Week Arrangement
Seven Nights of Sin

For a complete list of Kendall's books, visit:

www.kendallryanbooks.com/all-books/

Printed in Poland
by Amazon Fulfillment
Poland Sp. z o.o., Wrocław